This is the story of a woman who comes reluctantly to spirituality. Concerned about her guru-loving daughter, Ethel Katz is completely lovable, truly and charmingly drawn by Barbi Schulick, a gifted writer and explorer of the inner landscape. As we follow Ethel in her journey to understand her daughter, we see how the spiritual life can sneak up on a person, entering through the back door of skepticism and fear. *Ethel Katz Finds Her Guru* is a refreshing story about an anti-seeker who nevertheless finds. Ethel Katz teaches us about the enduring disconnect between what we chase and the deep yearning for peace. What you imagine for yourself, spiritually speaking, may be very different from what you end up with.
—JAN FRAZIER
author of *When Fear Falls Away* & *The Freedom of Being*

Who better to lead us down the road to the ashram than a lipsticked Jewish mother with a propensity for the pragmatic and a deep love for her spiritually-curious daughter? Uproariously funny, at turns powerfully poignant, *Ethel Katz Finds Her Guru* gives us the strength, humor and authenticity we need to find our divine humanity in the sometimes wild world of seekers and spiritual gurus. Ethel is unstoppable and Barbi Schulick's heart-stopping prose will carry you inexorably along to the novel's surprising, soul-changing finale.
—SUZANNE KINGSBURY
author of *The Summer Fletcher Greel Loved Me*

Ethel Katz Finds Her Guru

Ethel Katz Finds Her Guru

An UNLIKELY TALE *of* AWAKENING

Barbi Schulick

Epigraph Publishing Service
Rhinebeck, New York

Copyright © 2014 by Barbi Schulick

All rights reserved. No part of this book may be used or reproduced in any manner without written permission from the author except in reviews and critical articles. Contact the publisher for information.

This is a work of fiction. Names, characters, businesses, places, events and incidents are either the products of the author's imagination or used in a fictitious manner. Any resemblance to actual persons, living or dead, or actual events is purely coincidental.

Book design by Danielle Ferrara
Illustrations and author photo by Rosalie Schulick © 2014

Library of Congress Control Number: 2013955811
ISBN: 978-1-936940-67-7

Epigraph Books
22 East Market Street, Suite 304
Rhinebeck, NY 12572

Printed in the United States of America

For my mother,
who instilled me with humor and
common sense.

For Adyashanti,
who points the way.

The individual doesn't come here because of an intellectual
decision to come here.
Consciousness takes him by the ear and brings
him here. My next-door neighbors
don't come but people from all corners
of the world come here
with a sense of urgency. Why?

—NISARGADATTA MAHARAJ

One

Ethel Katz never wanted a guru. In fact, she didn't believe in such things. Why would anyone trust another person to know more about life than she could figure out herself? Ethel's daughter, Debra, on the other hand, had always been very interested in spiritual matters. When she was in high school she'd gone crazy over one of those Indian gurus and scared Ethel half to death. Then in college she hopped from one guru to another and traveled to Europe for some secret levitation course.

Ethel had been so worried she almost called a cult detective! Things settled down once Debra got married and started working at the newspaper and by the time Casey was born, she was almost back to normal. Now, with both kids in college, Debra was suddenly going off every few weekends for what she called "retreats," and this made Ethel nervous. What's she doing on these retreats? Every chance she and Fred get they run off to meditate with that new guru of theirs.

Ethel grabbed the dust cloth and polish from under the sink. She was cleaning up the condo before Fran, her old friend and neighbor, stopped by for coffee. What a way to spend the weekend, meditating all day. She angled the spray toward the dining-room table and paused to watch the foam bubble, taking in the familiar aroma. She swiped the cloth across the dark walnut, like they do in the commercial, then glanced down at the chair seats and brushed a few crumbs off their plastic-covered upholstery.

The buzzer sounded.

"Who's there?" Ethel barked into the intercom.

"Who do you think?" Fran barked back. Ethel chuckled and headed for the door.

"You smell like lemon," Fran said as she entered.

"I was polishing the table," said Ethel.

"Oh, you shouldn't have." They laughed and hugged. "The place looks nice. Is that new?" Fran pointed at a coat tree by the front door; Ethel's spring jacket and windbreaker dangled from the arched branches.

"I got tired of having to pry open the closet. It's a pain in the neck when the door gets stuck. How are you? You look thinner. Weight Watchers must be going well."

"Ounce by ounce."

"I envy your discipline," Ethel said, patting her bulging middle and noting that Fran's double chin had lost some of its heft. "Come, the coffee's ready. I only prepared fruit, so you're not tempted."

"Thanks." Fran slid into a chair while Ethel poured coffee into two mugs and brought out a fruit salad of cantaloupe, watermelon, and honeydew.

"Looks delicious," said Fran. "So how are things, Ethel?"

"Fine." Ethel took the seat across from Fran. "Nothing much new. Except that I've been worried about Debra lately. She found herself another guru."

"You're kidding. Since when? I thought she grew out of that years ago."

"The last few times I've visited I've noticed more and more books around by this fellow: Anandaji. Meshuggener, like the rest."

"Anandaji. An Indian person?" Fran served herself some fruit salad.

"No! He's American. With an Indian name. Did you ever hear of such a thing?"

"Just be happy she's not running away to Tibet like Sylvia Finkelstein's son. Remember her Alan shaved his head and joined a monastery? He's named Tinsle now or something like that."

"God forbid. I guess I should count my blessings. But I've had my own troubles with Debra." She rolled her eyes. "All of a sudden at sixteen she's a vegetarian. She wouldn't touch my pot roast and I had to lie and tell her there were no eggs in my noodle kugel. I used to sneak beef bouillon into my casseroles, just to get some extra protein into her." She dropped a teaspoon of sugar into her coffee and stirred.

"I remember coming over for dinner once and Debra was sitting at the table with her legs crossed like a pretzel. Milt tried to copy her but he couldn't get his legs up that high. He was some jokester." Fran sunk her fork into a wedge of honeydew.

Ethel glanced over at Milt's picture in a magnetic frame on the refrigerator and noticed the color was fading, making his features less distinct.

"Milt was more tolerant than I was. He trusted in Debra's good sense. But even he got concerned when she lost her accent. She started sounding like an Indian instead of a New Yorker."

"That's nutty." Fran popped a piece of watermelon into her mouth. The skin under her chin quivered slightly as she ate.

"I was so concerned; I snuck out to a meditation lecture once. I thought the guru would be there and I could get a look at him firsthand. Instead a local Jewish boy was speaking. Goldberg, I think. A little older than Debra. He was skinny as a rail and talked in that same singsong as Debra, smiling away as if he'd won the lottery. What was wrong with these kids?"

Fran leaned toward Ethel and patted her hand. "You put up with a lot of mishegas. And now she's at it again? I thought she'd straightened out for good."

"I thought so too. She's been eating like a normal person for years. Even improved on my chicken-soup recipe. She adds sweet potato. You ever try that?"

Fran shook her head, her mouth full of fruit.

"And she sent the kids to temple for a while. But I should have known from our conversations."

"What do you mean?" Fran topped off her coffee and wrapped her hands around her mug.

"Well, every now and then when I stay over at Debra's place until late, we talk. I ask her about her life, and she sometimes tells me how she feels about things. She talks about God in ways I don't understand."

"Like what?"

Ethel thought a minute. She took a few gulps of coffee. "I don't know. How we're all God, something like that. How God is inside everyone."

"That sounds pretty harmless. Even interesting."

"Yeah, but sometimes she'll get this look in her eyes that concerns me. Like from the hippie days. And if I say something about it she'll cut the conversation short. She's very touchy about God. I don't understand why. I mean, I believe in God. There must be a God. How did we get here otherwise? I just don't feel a need to think about it so much. You go to temple, you say a few prayers. That's enough."

Fran looked at her sympathetically. Most of her lipstick had washed away from the fruit, leaving a pale amber rim around the edge of her lips.

"Why can't she find a nice rabbi instead of a guru, for God's sake?" Ethel took another gulp of coffee. She was getting to the bottom of her cup and she savored the sugar that had settled there.

"That would be nice." Fran glanced at her watch. "I've gotta go, Ethel. Sorry to eat and run, but I promised Sophie Snider I'd check on her cat. She's away this week visiting her son. His wife left him. Poor thing."

"Oh, that's terrible! Okay, Fran, nice to see you. Would you like to take some fruit?"

"No, I had plenty. Thanks for the trouble."

Fran headed to the door and Ethel followed.

"I'll see you at bridge on Saturday," Ethel said.

"Yes, see you then." Fran patted Ethel's arm and kissed her cheek lightly, then waddled toward the door. Ethel noticed that her pants were hanging a little looser than usual.

While doing the dishes, Ethel eyed the brochure tucked under the phone book on the kitchen counter. She had snatched it from the magazine rack in Debra's bathroom. A flush of warmth passed over her cheeks. She'd never taken anything before, not without telling Debra. But she'd been so concerned. She wiped her hands and pulled out the brochure. The cover photograph displayed a spread of white clapboard buildings. A picture of the Buddha was in the far left corner under the address: Rte. One, South Amesburg, New York. South Amesburg. Ethel used to go there with Milt to see Jackie Mason. That's the Catskills, for God's sake! What's an ashram doing there? She opened the brochure and came face to face with a large picture of Anandaji, his blue eyes twinkling. Oy, what was the world coming to? She decided to go to South Amesburg to find out.

Two

LATE WEDNESDAY AFTERNOON ETHEL drove up the long entrance road to the ashram and pulled into the parking lot. Surveying the well-kept buildings and green grounds, she decided that except for the statue of a Buddha in the garden and the gathering of funny-looking sandals outside the meditation hall (those Birkenstock things Debra used to buy). "The Gateless Gate" looked much like the Catskill vacation spots she summered at with Milt. You'd barely know this place was an ashram, she thought.

She was pleased with the nicely spaced round tables in the dining hall, but wondered why some had signs marked "silent" in their centers. Still, the kitchen looked clean. She nodded approvingly at the fresh-faced workers wearing hairnets and chopping endless batches of vegetables.

Ethel didn't have a clue where to find Anandaji. At the main building a woman about Debra's age asked if she could help.

"I'd like to speak to Anandaji," she said, the request bordering on demand. The woman's eyes widened in surprise, and she smiled as if at some private joke.

Humph, was the guru too holy for visitors? She didn't like this woman. Her hair was a yellowish gray and too long for her age. A little color and the right cut would do a world of good.

"Have you prearranged a session with Anandaji?" the woman asked. Her voice was annoyingly soft.

"No," said Ethel. "No, I didn't. I didn't know it was necessary to prebook with a guru."

The woman met Ethel's glare with a dubious gaze.

"Anandaji doesn't often meet with people alone," she said. "There are too many of us. He asks that you write him a letter with your question and he may choose to address it in evening satsang."

"Evening what?" Ethel was irritated and dismayed.

"Satsang," answered the woman.

"What on earth is that?"

"Satsang means meeting in truth. It's another term for dharma talk."

Ethel stared at her, more confused than ever. Satsang. Dharma. These words sounded like the chants she used to hear coming from Debra's room when she was in high school. Once, Ethel knocked on her door and demanded to know what the words meant. Debra looked up at her, her face shining as she explained they were all names for God.

"God doesn't have a name!" blurted Ethel. "Not for the Jews, he doesn't! It's a sin to speak God's name!" She stormed out of the room before Debra could respond.

The woman at the reception desk handed Ethel a pen and a sheet of marigold paper inscribed with the words: Question for Anandaji.

"Dinner is at six and evening satsang is at seven thirty," she said. "You can leave Anandaji your question in the box outside the meditation hall."

She smiled sweetly, but Ethel wasn't falling for it. She stared at her, inspecting her mustache hairs.

"Can I get a room for the night?"

"Certainly," the woman said. "We have some nice single rooms on the main floor with a shared bath."

"I have to share a bath?"

"Well, we do have one single with a private bath left, but it's more expensive."

"I'll take it." Ethel handed the woman her credit card. *Share a bath? What does she think, I'm in college?*

Ethel found her way outside and down a path that led to the garden. A man was sitting very erect on a bench in front of the Buddha statue. He looked close to Ethel's age and was dressed quite reasonably in khaki pants and walking shoes. Ethel wondered what he was doing there. She took a seat at the opposite end of the garden near a bird bath, leaned her sheet of paper against her purse and wrote:

Dear Anandaji,

I have more than one question for you, so you'll forgive me if I surpass my quota.

First, why the question box? Don't the people who have deemed you holy deserve to speak to you face to face? I, by the way, am not one of those people. But my daughter, Debra, is. You may know her: Debra Wiener. She and her husband, Fred, keep coming here whenever they can get away. You probably see them more than I do. They came here last Rosh Hashanah instead of going to temple with me like they usually do. Debra said she'd feel closer to God here than she would in temple. I'll tell you, that hurt.

Here are some more questions for you, Mr. Anandaji. What do you think you have to teach my daughter? And why does she think she needs you? Life isn't so complicated, really. It's not always fun, but it's not complicated. You just have to make the best of things, be a good person, and try to enjoy yourself. I don't need a guru to tell me that. But I would appreciate if you could tell me why Debra thinks she does.

Sincerely,
Ethel Katz

Three

Ethel stood in her room wondering what a person wears to satsang. Was it like temple when you dress up? She eyed the one nice outfit she'd brought: a smart-fitting suit and her best pumps, but she doubted that was right. Most everyone she'd seen around the ashram was dressed casually—some a little more casually than she'd like, given the hippie types with matted hair and torn jeans. But most dressed much like she imagined Debra would if she were here: in cotton T-shirts, sweatshirts, and loose pants.

"I guess I'll wear my sweat suit, then." She suspected that no matter what she wore she'd look a little out of place. Her sweat suit was from her favorite boutique in Florida, where she spent her winters—bright pink with a silk-screened fish design. At the condo her neighbors always complimented her on how the pink matched her nail polish. She doubted that would happen here.

Ethel stepped into the sweatpants and felt the elastic tighten around her middle. She grimaced and examined herself in the mirror. She shouldn't have had that Sara Lee last night. She wondered what the desserts would be like at the ashram—probably those whole-wheat things. Feh.

Ethel looked at herself before putting the sweat-suit top on, noting the way her D-cup breasts ballooned at the edges in her Bali bra. She untangled the three gold chains around her neck and ran a comb through the frosted blonde tips of her cropped cut, inspecting the white roots barely visible at her part. She examined her reflection, making sure her mascara was sufficient. Normally she would reach for her lipstick and secure an extra coat, but she thought better of it. Au naturel in this place. What was she doing here? Debra would probably be upset if she knew. Still, Ethel took some pleasure in her chutzpah and couldn't deny the curiosity welling inside. She wanted to see this Anandaji.

At dinner Ethel chose the lentil loaf and salad, and passed on the miso soup and baked tofu. "No flavor in that stuff," she told the server whose eyes twinkled at her. Ethel smiled back, appreciating the solidarity, then chose a seat at a table already filled with people.

"How do you do? I'm Ethel Katz. I just drove up from Long Island," she said to them collectively. No one answered, save for a few nods and smiles. One young man lifted the silent sign from the middle of the table and held it out for her to see.

"Oh," she said. "Ohhh."

Did this mean she'd be eating in silence? She'd never done such a thing. You mean she had to just eat, surrounded by people, not even saying hello ... please pass the salt ... nice salad dressing? Across from her the woman from the main building was wrapped in a shawl and sipping her miso soup. Next to her, a boxy, middle-aged man seemed to be praying over his food. Oy vey. Ethel poked her lentil loaf with her fork, wishing she was at her favorite deli, eating a nice pastrami sandwich.

At seven, Ethel filed into the spacious hall behind a trail of others, who, bowing as they entered, walked slowly and silently through the carpeted aisles. She grabbed one of the chairs toward the back. She certainly wasn't going to sit on one of those odd little cushions in the front of the hall. Most people sat very straight, some with their eyes closed. No one talked. At the head of the hall next to a table holding a statue of the Buddha and a pitcher of water, was the most comfortable-looking seat in the place. And walking toward it was Anandaji.

He looked like his picture—a man, about forty-five, with a shaved head, wearing a tunic and beads—but he was smaller than Ethel thought he'd be, and skinnier. No meat on his bones. No wonder with the food they serve here. Anandaji sat and gazed out at the group. Ethel was taken aback. He was ... so attractive! It wasn't that his features were that unusual, but there was something extraordinary about him that Ethel couldn't put her finger on. It was as if lights were shining inside his blue eyes; he seemed to sparkle with happiness. She found herself smiling at him for no reason at all.

Anandaji poured himself some water and began to talk. His voice was pleasant, not deep, not high, and his manner was nothing like she expected. He could have been a friendly bus driver or the man who takes her dry cleaning, or her gardener, or dentist. There was simply nothing guruish about him. But what he talked about—that was different.

"Today we're going to consider the question, who am I?" said Anandaji. "We think we are all sorts of things—our bodies, our names, the roles we play: mother, friend, husband. But mostly, we think we're our thoughts, our opinions of ourselves and others, our beliefs and ideas. But, who are you, really?" said Anandaji. "Look and see. Look beyond your thoughts. What do you find? Don't look for an answer. Who you really are isn't something you can know with your mind. It's something you are being. It is being itself."

While Anandaji talked, Ethel leaned toward him in her seat, not because she couldn't hear him, but because she didn't understand him. And the fact that she couldn't understand him confused her even more than what he was saying. She considered herself an intelligent person. He wasn't using such fancy language, but what he was saying, all this stuff about who she really was. What was he talking about? And how did Anandaji know better than Ethel who she was?

As far as Ethel could tell, she was Ethel—daughter of Tillie and Morris, wife of Milt for thirty-eight years, mother of Debra. She'd always lived in New York. She drove a Volvo; she liked to play bridge. She was a Jew and proud of it. And a Democrat, though she did vote for Bloomberg in the last election. She was a good, kind person who cared about the people in her life. Just last week she brought her neighbor Doris a casserole after her hip surgery. And every now and then she put in a few hours for the March of Dimes. If that wasn't who she was ... then who was she? The thought drew a blank and made her mind dizzy. She looked around the room to see if anyone else understood more than she did. Many people were nodding quietly to themselves with serene looks on their faces. Others had their eyes closed and seemed to be drinking in Anandaji's words.

A woman a few rows ahead of Ethel raised her hand to ask a question. Anandaji nodded and the woman walked to a microphone in the center aisle. She was short with wavy, black hair and an intelligent voice. After she greeted Anandaji, she gazed at him for a few moments. Ethel fidgeted in her chair. Why the love fest? He was a nice looking man. Maybe she had a crush. Ethel thought she could see tears in the woman's eyes.

"Lately, Anandaji," the woman began, "I can't tell where I end and the rest of the world begins."

Anandaji nodded.

"I mean, of course I'm aware of my body, but it doesn't seem any longer that my body, or even my mind, contain me. There's much more presence—inside and out. I seem to be flowing through life, like I'm part of its essence, like I'm made of the same stuff."

Ethel shifted in her seat. What kind of cockamamy story was that? She hoped Debra didn't start in with this. Where she begins and where she ends? Ethel knew where she began and ended—at her head and her feet! Just like everyone else. Ethel waited for Anandaji to respond, but instead he thanked the woman for sharing and looked back at her, as if in some private communication. When the woman sat back down, he picked up a stack of marigold question sheets on the table beside him. Ethel covered her mouth with her hands. Much to her surprise, she was afraid that one of those sheets of paper contained her letter and that Anandaji would share it with the whole group. She realized now that hers were not the typical questions that people asked in satsang.

Anandaji read one sheet silently and then chuckled. Uh oh, that's gotta be me. But then he said, "Henry, you want to come up and talk about this?" Ethel relaxed back into her seat and stared blankly at the sky-colored wall behind Anandaji. A series of barely distinguishable ink drawings hung in a row, something with a man and an ox. Henry rose from a cushion toward the front of the room and headed to the mike. Ethel saw that he was the man in khakis from the garden. She was surprised a man his age could sit on one of those cushions. Didn't his knees hurt?

"Hi Anandaji," Henry said in a Brooklyn accent.

"Hey, Henry," said Anandaji. Ethel could tell Anandaji liked Henry. There was no gazing this time.

"So, Anandaji," said Henry. "I understand intellectually what you're talking about—that we're not really our names or the roles we play in life, that our essential nature, the Buddha nature, is beyond all that, nameless and empty. Still, as far as I can tell, I'm just Henry, 5'9", from Brooklyn, balding, a pretty nice guy. You know, Henry."

Laughter rose through the group and Ethel found herself chuckling along. As the laughter died down, Anandaji said, "So you know, Henry, these attributes you listed, your name, height, residence, how much hair you have (more laughter) are just concepts of who you are."

"Yes," said Henry. "I get that."

"And," said Anandaji, "even the deeper values that seem to define you—who you love, how you believe people should behave, political opinions, your Buddhist beliefs ... can you see that these are concepts too, systems of thought you've taken on as your own?"

"Yes," said Henry, nodding. "That's harder, but yes, I can see that."

"So," said Anandaji. "Who are you without those things?"

Henry waited before answering. Ethel watched him, really interested now. Here was a man who could have been in her bridge group, or on the temple planning board, standing and asking a guru who he was. She never could have dreamed of such a thing. But more interesting to Ethel, was that Henry was asking about something Ethel had just been wondering about herself.

Henry cleared his throat and talked slowly. "Anandaji, I really don't know how to answer. I don't get an answer. My mind is blank. I don't know who I am without those things."

"Precisely," said Anandaji. "That's a very good place to be. The mind is confounded. It can't imagine who it is without its concepts. The funny part is that even though the mind is hard at work trying to figure this out, this is exactly what it can't figure out. The mind is not who you are, even though it thinks it is. This isn't about knowing something in the way the mind is accustomed to. It's about not knowing."

Henry nodded thoughtfully, thanked Anandaji, and walked back to his cushion. Ethel shot him a perplexed glance. She'd lost Anandaji's reasoning early on and now she wondered what Henry was thinking. A man his age. She clucked her tongue. A nice man like that, falling for a guru. She looked around the room. Everyone seemed calm, as if they were perfectly content and wouldn't want to be anywhere else. She studied the statue of the Buddha next to Anandaji and wondered about the peaceful look those statues always had. That little smile like the Mona Lisa. As if he were enjoying a secret no one else knew.

Four

When Ethel got back to her room after satsang, it was only nine thirty. She decided to give Debra a call. She couldn't keep the fact that she was at the ashram a secret forever, and she figured she might as well get it over with. She pulled on her nightgown, put on some hand cream, checked the polish on her nails for wear, and got out her cell phone. She had a weak signal. If this place were really the Catskills, there'd be a phone in the room. She tested the signal near the window by the bed and it went up a few notches. She sat on the edge of the bed and dialed.

"Hello?" said Debra.

'Hi, dear," said Ethel.

"Oh, hi, Ma. You on your cell? Where are you?"

"I'm in South Amesburg."

Debra paused. "What do you mean? You're in the Catskills?"

"No. Well, yes. But no."

"Well, where are you then? You sound strange, Ma."

"I'm at the ashram, dear. Anandaji's." She glanced at the ashram brochure sitting on the night table. A miniature Anandaji smiled up at her.

"What? What do you mean you're at the ashram? How did you even know where it was?" Ethel could hear her say to Fred in a loud whisper, "My mother's at the ashram!"

"I found the leaflet in your bathroom. I was interested."

"You were interested? Since when are you interested, Ma? I can't believe this. Since when are you interested?"

"Well, since you got involved. His books are all over your house. You and Fred are rushing out here every chance you get. I wanted to see what the big deal was."

This time there was a longer pause, after which Debra made a few attempts to speak. "Ma," was all she could manage.

"I had a genuine interest," said Ethel. She fiddled with an unraveling thread on the quilted bedspread.

"No," Debra said, rallying. "You didn't have a genuine interest. You had a genuine need to meddle. To make sure I wasn't doing anything dangerous, right?"

Ethel could hear Fred laughing in the background.

"Well, maybe."

"Unbelievable. You're unbelievable, Mom. You know, I'm not eighteen anymore."

"That's true. But that doesn't mean you always know what's best for you."

There was dead silence on the other end of the phone.

"Debra, I'm sorry if I've offended you. I was truly concerned."

"I'm going to try very hard to believe that. I really am."

"If Casey did something that concerned you, you'd look into it, wouldn't you?" Ethel leaned into the cellphone receiver, as if asking it the question.

"Casey is eighteen years old."

"I know. I realize this must seem odd."

"To say the least." Debra took a big sigh. "So, what do you think? Am I in danger of losing my soul to Anandaji?"

Ethel picked up the brochure and peered at Anandaji's photograph, then flipped it face down on the night table.

"Probably not. But I don't see what's so great about him. He's just a regular man in a tunic."

Debra laughed and repeated what Ethel said to Fred, who howled.

"I mean everyone is so starry-eyed. It's ridiculous," Ethel went on, encouraged. "And all this talk about enlightenment and finding out who you really are. It's silly. We are who we are."

"Oh yeah? And who might that be?" said Debra.

"Don't start in."

"I'm not starting in. I'm asking you a question. You're there at the ashram, aren't you?

"Debra, I know who I am."

"Yeah?"

"Yes. I'm your mother."

"Okay. You're my mother. I can't believe you did this. I just can't believe it. So what did you do so far?"

"I went to dinner where no one talked and I ate beans that gave me gas."

Debra laughed. "What else? Did you go to satsang?"

"Yes, satsang. With the uncomfortable chairs, or those pillows. Do you sit on those pillows?"

"Yes, I do."

"Everyone's younger than me on those pillows. Except for one man. He's Jewish, I think, from Brooklyn. Henry."

"Oh, sure, I know Henry. He comes with his son, Phil. Henry's great."

"Henry's great?"

"Yeah, I like him a lot. Very genuine."

"He seems a little mixed up to me," said Ethel. Debra didn't answer. Ethel noticed the heat coming from her cell phone and shifted it to her other ear. "I just don't understand why these people think they need to come here and moon all over a teacher," she said. "Why do you need to come here, Debra?"

Debra sighed. "I guess it's just always been that way for me, Mom. You know that." She paused. "Don't you ever wonder what life is all about?"

"You sound like that song." Ethel hummed a few bars.

"Yeah, that's it. What's It All about, Alfie? Don't you ever wonder, Ma?"

"Well yes, now and then. I imagine everybody does. I remember Daddy once bought a book about past lives. We joked that he might have been my wife once, and I told him I couldn't imagine him cooking a decent meal!" She laughed and thought about Debra on the end of the line, laughing with her. She was relieved she was settling down. "Do you think there are past lives?" she asked.

"Sure," Debra said. "I was probably your mother once."

"Very funny." Ethel thought a moment, smoothing her hand over the bedspread. "Well even if it's true, I don't understand why you need a guru to tell you. What makes people think Anandaji knows what life's all about?"

"There have always been people who understand life more than the rest of us," Debra told her. "Buddha, Mohammed, Abraham, Jesus."

"Jesus was a Jew."

"Yes, Mom, I know. There are plenty in Judaism, rabbis like the Baal Shem Tov. People who uncovered the …" Debra hesitated. "The truth of who we are."

"The truth of who we are," repeated Ethel. "I'm not sure I understand what you're talking about, but if this truth is who we are, then why don't we all just know it?"

This time Debra paused a long time. Ethel waited and looked out the window. A man with a pensive look on his face walked slowly down the road. Finally Debra said softly, "I think we forget it. Or maybe we get distracted. It's hard to explain. I'm not sure I'm saying the right things. It's a good question, though. It's a really good question." She was quiet. Then she laughed. "I can't believe I'm saying this, but why don't you ask Anandaji?"

Ethel grumbled. But she thought to herself, Maybe I will.

Five

THE NEXT MORNING ETHEL woke up surprised to find herself still at the ashram. She'd dreamed of home. She thought that was probably where she should be, but if she was going to meet Anandaji, she'd have to stay. She considered her dental cleaning tomorrow and the bridge game coming up. If she stayed she'd better hold her daily paper and mail; they'd be piling up at the door. Glancing at her suitcase she felt pleased she'd had the foresight to bring some extra things, but did she really want to stay? Despite her uncertainty, she found herself searching for phone numbers in her address book, calling the newspaper first, then the post office, and then the dentist. Finally she called Fran, who was perturbed to have to find a bridge sub and asked Ethel far too many questions about her whereabouts. Ethel had to think fast, rationalizing that it was better to tell a white lie, than to have the whole bridge group talking about her. She'd never known Fran to keep a secret. She cursed her bad luck at not getting her answering machine.

"I'm … in the city, Fran. Visiting a cousin of Milt's. She's under the weather." Ethel was a poor liar and Fran suspected something.

"What? Milt's cousin? You never mentioned such a person. This couldn't wait until after the game? We've been doing so well."

"It's important." Ethel stammered off the phone, her heart racing. What was she doing? Lying and passing up bridge for a guru? She couldn't find an answer.

At breakfast she settled for oatmeal and honey, and curled her lip at a tray of scrambled tofu. What, they never heard of eggs? Ethel sat alone at a small table. Fewer people came to breakfast, and most ate in silence, some with eyes cast toward their food, others gazing around the room smiling, as if they'd never seen anything so wonderful as the ashram dining hall. What a bunch. Ethel shook her head, vaguely wondering if she might be missing something.

At morning satsang, Anandaji announced that he'd be leading a meditation. He asked the group to sit comfortably. Fat chance on this chair, thought Ethel, shifting her weight on the thinly cushioned seat in the back row, and envying Anandaji, who appeared perfectly comfortable sitting cross-legged and straight-backed at the front of the hall.

"So, even before we begin what we call silent meditation," Anandaji said, "I'd like you to consider what meditation really is and whether there is actually anywhere to go when you close your eyes. Is there any particular state to seek? What is it we're really looking for? The obvious answer for most spiritual seekers is that we're looking for quietness. For peace. For stillness. For being. But before you start looking, I want you to ask yourself, Is there anything to find that isn't already here? Isn't quietness already here? And stillness? And being? Isn't being always here?"

Anandaji went on this way for a while and then started taking longer pauses between his sentences. He asked the group to gently notice their thoughts and any noises or physical sensations, and just allow it all to flow along, being with whatever was there, moment to moment.

Ethel had never meditated before and she wondered if she was really meditating now. All this seemed like was sitting quietly, and uncomfortably, while thinking. She thought about Debra and what meditating might be like for her, imagining it was probably more enjoyable than what Ethel was doing, or else Debra wouldn't want to do it so often. She thought about how she'd never really thought about meditation before and how she'd never asked Debra to explain it to her. She thought about Anandaji's voice and how soothing it sounded, but also how confusing his words were, how she wasn't sure what he meant by "being." She couldn't imagine that this was really meditation. This couldn't be what all the hoopla was about. She thought about lunch and how she hoped they'd at least have some cheese, something besides tofu or beans. For a while she listened to the labored breathing of an overweight woman a few rows behind her, finding it, in turns, annoying and entertaining. Then out of the blue, she thought about Milt, and how amazed he'd be that she was here. For a long while, she thought about Fran and how she didn't buy Ethel's story about being in the city. She would probably tell the bridge group that

Ethel was acting strangely. And then, toward the end of the meditation time, without warning, her thoughts became distant and vague. For a few moments it seemed like she was sleeping, except that she knew she was awake. A gentle breeze came through a nearby window.

"Soon we'll open our eyes," said Anandaji, "but before you do, consider the fact that the meditation doesn't have to end here. This simplicity of allowing everything to be as it is, of not looking for anything to be different, of seeing that whatever peace you're wishing was here is actually already here; this ease is present even in active life and can follow you through your day. It's there at the ground of all experience."

Ethel's eyes popped open when Anandaji finished talking. She was surprised at how alert she felt. How could that be just from sitting and thinking? She turned to the person next to her: a girl in her twenties who smiled, then bent over in her chair and grabbed her toes to stretch out her back. The man in front of her was rolling his head, loosening up his neck muscles. Like Debra with all that yoga.

The morning satsang wasn't much different than the night before. More questions about who you are and what life is and more answers that made no sense to Ethel. This time Anandaji went on for a while about the oneness of the universe and how there's really only one thing happening and that we're really not separate from each other. A woman got up to say that as hard as she tried, she still didn't get it. Anandaji told her it was the trying that was stopping her from getting it, and not to worry about it, getting it would just come and in truth, there was nothing to get. Everyone laughed at this and Ethel thought, if there's nothing to get, what is everyone doing here?

On the way to lunch, Ethel noticed Henry a few paces in front of her, heading to the dining hall. He was walking with a younger, taller man who moved with the same leisurely strides as Henry. She quickened her pace to catch up with them.

"Hello," she said, "I'm Ethel Katz. I'm Debra Wiener's mother. She said she knows you."

Henry seemed startled at first, but then stopped walking, smiled, and introduced himself and Phil, adding, "Debra, and her husband, Fred, right? They come weekends sometimes. Nice people. What brings you to the ashram?"

"I just wanted to see what it was all about. Debra seems so excited about this place." Ethel felt a stab of guilt, recalling Debra's accusation that she was meddling.

"What do you think so far?" Henry asked. He and Phil gazed at Ethel earnestly. Henry's eyes were a watery blue and Phil's large and brown, but they had the same crescent moon eyebrows and doorknob nose. Both were lanky with long, graceful fingers, Henry's with a few liver spots, she noted while considering what to say.

"It's interesting," was all she could come up with. They both threw back their heads and laughed. "What do you think of it?" she asked, looking at Henry.

"Me? Oh." He paused an uncomfortably long time, looking past her, not really thinking, it seemed, just pausing. "My wife, Sil, died a year ago." Henry's voice was softer now. "I lost my reason to live. Anandaji helped bring me back. This place is my refuge. I found something…" He paused again. "Something I never realized was possible."

Ethel wanted to know what that was, but she stopped herself from asking. She knew how it felt to be newly widowed. It took her years to regain herself after Milt died. She didn't want to irritate fresh wounds for Henry, but she also sensed that whatever he'd found with Anandaji was different than the rallying back into life she'd finally achieved after mourning Milt.

She felt a touch on her arm and turned to see the woman from the main building, her yellow-gray hair catching a gleam of sunlight.

"Hello, Ethel," she said, "I have a message for you from Anandaji. He'd like to meet with you this afternoon. He'll expect you at two.

"He wants to see me?" She pointed to herself.

The woman nodded. "He lives in the first bungalow at the top of the hill that leads away from the main entrance." Ethel recalled noticing that hilly road when she parked her car. She watched the woman walk away, her lavender scarf flowing behind her. Ethel looked at Phil and Henry, who smiled, flashing the same square front teeth.

"Lucky you," said Phil.

Ethel wasn't so sure.

Six

Ethel stood in front of the bathroom mirror trying to will away the nervous flutter in her belly. Why she felt anxious about seeing Anandaji, she couldn't figure. She fiddled with her hair, coaxing an errant slice of bangs into place, then slathered her amber blush on either cheek. She even considered touching up her nails, but stopped herself. "It's not a date, for God's sake!"

It was only one fifteen and she had no idea what to do with herself until two. She hadn't brought along any reading material, and her trip through that silly ashram bookstore had revealed only books by teachers like Anandaji, and gurus from India and Tibet, whom Ethel found even more daunting than he was. All this stuff about having no self. How could you have no self? It's crazy! And doesn't anyone at this place wonder what's going on in the world? No newspapers, no television. What's wrong with these people? She should just leave. If she left now she'd be back for the bridge game and could see if Fran would want to have dinner first at that new fish place. She could go for a nice piece of salmon. But when Ethel grabbed her cell phone and sat on her bed to dial Fran's number, her fingers dialed Debra's work number instead.

"Debra Wiener."

"Hi dear."

"Hi Mom. You on your cell phone again?" Debra sounded a little anxious, as if she'd been waiting to hear from her. "Are you still at the ashram?"

"Yes, but I'm getting tired of it. This place is not for me."

Debra laughed.

"What's so funny?"

"Mom, we both know the ashram's not for you. I'm surprised you've lasted this long."

Ethel was quiet. She could hear Debra rustling papers.

"What's wrong, Mom?"

"Well, I'm supposed to see Anandaji today. At two."

"What? You're kidding. You mean, see him privately?"

"Yeah." She found the loose thread on her bedspread and twirled it around her finger.

"Geez, he doesn't do that too often. How'd that happen?"

"It just did."

"Oh, c'mon, Mom. Did you put in a question or something?"

"Yes."

"What'd you ask?"

"Well, I asked about you." She pulled the thread a little tighter.

"You're kidding. Tell me you didn't do that."

"You don't have to worry. I didn't say anything personal."

"I'm not worried. I don't care if it's personal. It's not that." She paused. "It's the way you'd represent me, I guess." She paused again. "But it's okay. I can deal with it. So what did you ask?"

"I asked him why you think you need him so much, why anyone needs him, but at this point, I'm not sure I really want to know. I'm very confused."

She untwirled the thread and smoothed it into the bedspread. She looked at the picture over her bed: a snow-covered mountain reflected in a glistening lake.

"That's the same question you asked me. It seems to be on your mind. You should talk to him about it."

"Maybe."

"Mom, you shouldn't leave now that you're there. It's very special to be with Anandaji."

"Why? Why is it so special? What's so great about him?"

"Can't you tell yet? Tell the truth."

Ethel didn't answer. In the distance someone was talking on the phone in Debra's office.

"Mom?"

"Okay, he may have something special, but I can't tell what it is. He's just a person. Maybe it's all the fanfare about him that makes people think he's important."

"I think it's more than that. There must be a reason people want to be around him so much, don't you think?"

"Well, I'm not one of those people. I'm ready to get out of this place. It's okay for you and Fred and the rest of them, but not me." She picked at a hangnail on her thumb. "Have you ever talked to Anandaji?"

"Well, not alone, but, yes, I've talked to him. Up at the mike."

"What was that like, in front of all those people?"

"You kind of forget about the people. Or you don't care they're there. It's nice they're there. What's important is asking him something from your heart and looking at him, taking in his words."

Ethel's pitch hiked up a notch. "You're talking cuckoo, Debra. Like the rest of them. Look at him. Taking in his words, as if whatever he says is perfect."

"Look Mom, it wasn't my idea you go there. I could be really mad at you for this. I don't need my mother checking out my spiritual teacher for God's sake."

"Okay, okay. I'm sorry. It's just that you make him sound like he's a god or something." She peeled off the hangnail, leaving a red mark.

"I know it sounds that way, but it's not. Anandaji is just a person, but he's also different than most people. He's more ... empty."

"Empty?" She glanced at the ashram brochure she'd left face down on the night table.

"He's in touch with the part of himself that has no ego. He's not motivated by his ego. Do you know what I mean?"

"You mean he's very nice? Kind-hearted? I know plenty of people like that. Your father was like that. Some of the time. And your Aunt Shirl. Not a mean bone in her body. But people weren't lining up at the door to stare into her eyes."

"It's not like Aunt Shirl, Ma." Debra sighed. "It's hard to explain without using all those words that make it sound like something it's not."

"What do you mean? What words?" Ethel brushed away some hairs from her latex pillow, feeling pleased she'd brought it along.

"Well, like enlightened. You could say Anandaji's enlightened."

"Oh, yes, enlightened. So what does that mean, anyway?" She picked up the brochure and looked at Anandaji's photo, then put it face down again.

"That's a good question. People are pretty mixed up about what it means. At least that's what Anandaji says. But the way he usually puts it is that enlightenment means you're sort of untethered from ego. You identify less with the personal and more with the universal."

"Like Mother Teresa?"

"Maybe."

"I just don't like treating people like some sort of god."

"All I know is that when I'm with him—and it doesn't have to be at the ashram, it can be at home reading one of his books, or listening to a tape while I'm driving to work—when I bring him into my life, I feel more at home with myself and everything else. There's this feeling of peace. But, isn't it getting late? Shouldn't you go? It's a bit of a hike up to Anandaji's bungalow."

Ethel looked at her watch. 1:47 p.m. "Yes dear. I'd better leave."

"Let me know how it goes. Geez, Mom, I can't believe it. You are some crazy lady."

"Yes, I guess I am."

Ethel navigated around the ashram campus toward the dirt road up to Anandaji's. She kept a steady pace, happy she was wearing her walking shoes. The air was fresh and the grounds were spread with wildflowers and ferns. Chickadees gathered at a feeder outside the staff housing. She watched them in their little black caps, cracking open sunflower seeds against the branches. She recalled what Debra had said about feeling peaceful around Anandaji. She didn't need a guru to feel peaceful. She could just look at these birds. She headed up the hill, thinking back to a trip she took to the Caribbean with Milt and how the water felt like silk over her shoulders. That was peace.

But deep down, she suspected that Debra was talking about something more than that. Last night Anandaji had said that a person could feel peace no matter what was happening: driving in traffic or having a hard day at work; visiting a sick friend or watching upsetting news. How was that possible? And what is this enlightenment thing? What did Debra say? Untethered from your ego? Why would anyone want that? Isn't it important to have an ego? What would she be without one? She might act a little wacky. Ethel felt a surge of alarm for Debra. Oy, what's wrong with that girl, always getting involved with these crazy things. First Baba what's-his-name. Then that hugging lady from India, and now this Anandaji.

At the thought of his name, Ethel pictured his funny clean-shaven head and those sparkling eyes. She couldn't help but smile. He's not so bad, really. Her stomach fluttered as she reached the final rise in the road and a bungalow came into view. Outside, Anandaji was on his knees, pulling weeds in his garden. He looked just like anybody gardening on a sunny afternoon. He looked like anybody at all.

Seven

As ETHEL NEARED THE BUNGALOW, Anandaji spotted her and stood, waving her toward him.

"Hello," he said, when she was near. "Ethel, right?" He smiled warmly, his hands folded in front of him, his T-shirt smudged with dirt.

"Yes." Ethel was pleased that he knew her name.

"I'd shake hands, but I'm a little dirty," he said, opening his soil-darkened palms for her to inspect.

She nodded and chuckled. "You like gardening?"

"Love it. So hey, let's go around back. There's a nice deck. Would you like some tea?"

He's very nice, thought Ethel, following him.

"Yes, thank you," she said. "Though I'm not much for that herbal stuff they have at the dining hall."

"Me neither," said Anandaji. "I keep Earl Grey at the house. That okay?" He pointed to a pot already set on a small table between two Adirondack chairs.

"Wonderful." She sat down and watched Anandaji rinse off his hands with a hose, then wave them in the air to dry. He poured the tea and handed her a cup. She breathed in the steam and smiled. There was something distinctly familiar about him. In a flash she realized he reminded her of her nephew, Solomon, her brother Alfred's son. Sol had always been close to Ethel and like a brother to Debra. He grew up a few blocks away from them. A busy lawyer in the city, he visited Ethel whenever he was home and he still called her Auntie. But Sol was dark and tall, so it wasn't their looks. Ethel noted the blond stubble on Anandaji's head and how neatly his small frame folded into his chair. But it was something.

Anandaji took a long sip of tea and smacked his lips "Sure does beat that herbal stuff," he said, smiling.

That's it! That smile, so … playful. And the way it made her feel: warm and comfortable.

A flurry of chickadees alighted on a feeder hanging from a nearby tree. Their song pierced the air and Anandaji mimicked them. "Chickadee-dee-dee," he sang, then laughed when they answered. Ethel liked the way his whole body shook like a child when he laughed. So absorbed in the birds Anandaji seemed to have forgotten Ethel, but then he turned to her and said, "I liked your letter. You're very honest."

"I'm not sure Debra would be so happy about it."

"Maybe not," said Anandaji, "but you didn't write it for Debra, did you?"

Ethel thought for a moment. "Well, I don't know," she said, uncertain of what he meant. "I've felt a little concerned about her when it comes to these groups … and gurus."

"Is she concerned?"

"Well no. She's perfectly happy."

Anandaji grinned, then took a sip of tea, his eyes on Ethel.

"You think I should lay off," said Ethel, with a mixture of annoyance and chagrin. Her back stiffened. She balanced at the edge of her seat.

"I think you may want to look at where your concern is coming from."

"What do you mean?"

"Is your concern really for Debra? Or for yourself?"

Ethel shifted from side to side. She wasn't sure she liked where this was going. "Why did you change your name?" she blurted. "You're an American boy, for God's sake. What are you doing with an Indian name?"

Anandaji laughed out loud. "You're funny," he said.

"I didn't mean to be. I really want to know. It seems such a silly, unnecessary thing, this one name business. What does it say on your passport, your license?"

"It says, Anandaji." He shrugged.

Ethel waited for more, but none came. "You mean like Cher?"

He laughed again. "Kind of like that, I guess."

"What was your old name? The one your parents gave you?"

"Robert."

"Now that's a nice name. I was going to name Debra Robert if she was a boy." Ethel took her first sip of tea.

"Oh?"

"Yes. Now why on earth would you want to be Anandaji instead of Robert?" She leaned back in her chair.

Anandaji laughed again, but then said quietly, "My teacher gave me my name."

"You had a teacher?"

"Yes." His eyes remained on Ethel.

Ethel looked back. Anandaji's expression grew thoughtful. They stopped talking for what seemed like a while. She realized this wouldn't happen with most people, to stop talking in the middle of a conversation. The longer she was silent, the calmer she felt, and the less interested she became in Anandaji's name. It no longer seemed important, or even fair, to press him on the subject.

A chickadee sounded nearby and Anandaji laughed.

"I love those birds," he said. "Look, on that branch." She followed his finger. The bird perched on a nearby apple tree. "Ethel, what do you call that bird?"

"That's a chickadee. A black-capped chickadee. See its funny head—like a black cap?"

"But what would you call it if you didn't know its name?"

Ethel thought. "Well, I'd just call it a bird."

"And what if you didn't have the word for bird? What if you'd never been taught the word, bird? What would you call it then?"

Ethel didn't answer. Her thoughts darted around as she tried to make sense of what Anandaji was asking. She wondered how they got onto this subject.

"What I mean," said Anandaji, "is what is a name really, but a meaningless sound, a vocal expression we use to represent something. But the thing itself, what's that? What's a bird? What's a bird without its name?"

"You mean, what if I'd never learned language, like a baby?"

"Yes, exactly. What is it then?" Anandaji had that Sol smile again.

"Well, I don't know," she said slowly. "I don't know what a bird is." Ethel felt a little light-headed saying this. She slid to the edge of the chair and sat up straight.

"Precisely," said Anandaji. "We don't know what a bird is. Bird. Chickadee. They mean nothing. They're only symbols that try to explain the unexplainable. Robert. Anandaji. Same thing."

"Oh, I see," said Ethel, though she wasn't sure she did. A memory flashed. She was six years old, spending the day collecting shells on the beach at Coney Island. Sitting in the sand inspecting them, she held a wide clamshell in her palm and delighted at the smooth, pink mother-of-pearl sheen of its inside. Gliding her fingertips over it, absorbed in its gloss and shimmer, the shell suddenly seemed like something magical, something from another world, unknown and mysterious. That must be what he was talking about.

"Anandaji, why do people come here to be with you?"

"Beats me." They both laughed. Anandaji crossed a leg over his knee. Ethel noticed he was wearing worn-out running shoes, probably reserved for garden work. "It's because they're looking for something," he said. "They're seekers. Seekers never rest. They think I have what they're looking for."

"Do you?" Ethel asked.

"I don't have anything they don't have themselves," said Anandaji.

"You'll forgive me for asking then. Do you really think you can teach them something?"

"No," said Anandaji. "I don't. I can only remind them of what they already know. We all hold the truth inside."

Looking out at the mountains in the distance, Ethel pondered this. She knew about trusting convictions and acting on what was right, but Anandaji seemed to be talking about something more. She'd heard him talk about this "truth" in satsang—as if there was some enormous truth that governed the whole world and everyone had access to it. She remembered him saying that this truth was who she already was. She wondered if this was so, and why it wasn't easier to understand; why people needed someone like Anandaji to explain it. But she didn't care to ask any more questions. There was something about being with Anandaji that made her want to be quiet. The trees, the air, the birds, the way he reminded her of Sol, it was almost like being alone on a really good day, a feeling in her body, as if she'd lost weight, or just taken a long bath. But it was even more peaceful than that, just like Debra said.

Eight

THAT EVENING THERE WAS an extra long meditation scheduled before satsang and Ethel decided not to go. What good is sitting there doing nothing for an hour? She stood in the hallway outside the meditation hall watching one person after another remove their shoes, shuffle to their cushions, wrap themselves in shawls, uncreak their necks, straighten their postures, and close their eyes. Many had blissful smiles on their faces as if absorbed in a happy daydream, others shifted around unable to get comfortable. Some yawned. One man by the far wall was weeping. Ethel couldn't help thinking they were wasting their time. Why don't they just go for a walk? It's such a nice night. Or take a nap if they're tired. And that sad one needs someone to talk to. She clucked her tongue and headed for the garden.

She returned to the seat near the birdbath where she'd first composed her letter to Anandaji. The sound of the little waterfall relaxed her. She'd saved a cookie from dinner to munch on. Oatmeal-raisin with far too much whole-wheat flour, and honey instead of sugar. About halfway through, she laid it down on the bench, annoyed. Yech, it's like a rock. Enough already with the wholesome ingredients. Ethel thought fondly of her bakery back home—the rugelach and black-and-white cookies, her favorite pound cake that she served for bridge. She thought for the hundredth time how she should go home. She wasn't so worried about Debra anymore, so why stay? But this time she had to face the fact that for some crazy reason she had gone ahead and secured her room through the weekend. She looked at the waterfall and her mind grew quiet, listening to the gurgle of the water and her steady breathing. She thought she might fall asleep, except that she was interested and focused on the things around her: the soft gray air of the night, the fresh smell of mint from the garden, the banter and clanging of kitchen workers trailing from the dining hall. Her body felt unusually still, much like it had with Anandaji.

She guessed this was what it was all about, why people came here. She was so quiet, so peaceful, it made her wonder if she'd turn into a real loony and never leave. She laughed out loud at this and then a surge of alarm shot through her. Her face grew warm. Oh dear, what if this is how it happens? Her mind raced over the events of the day. What if this was a cult? The guru invites you to his house and puts a spell over you. He offers you your favorite tea. He has a nice smile; he seems perfectly harmless; he's just an ordinary guy. But then he asks you strange questions. He hypnotizes you. He hypnotized her! That's what was going on! Thump, thump. Oh no. She was standing and waving her hands like a fan near her face. Pop would kill her. Oh God, Pop. I'm sorry. She sat down. What was she doing? It was so strange here. She stared into the night. The breeze was cool against her face. Her heart settled a bit.

Pop. She hadn't thought of him in so long. His ruddy face, the white stubble of beard, pale blue eyes and strong nose, the way he used her pet name, Madala, and called her to him to join in the evening prayers when she was a girl. Sometimes they'd sing the Hebrew together. His voice was high and filled the room. His eyelids quivered while he swayed under his prayer shawl. It was like he was in a trance and took her with him to some faraway place. She'd close her eyes too and travel deep into the Hebrew. Eliyahu Hanave. Eliyahu Hatishbe. Pop. Why was she thinking of him? Why did she feel like he was there?

"Are you okay? Can I help?" A voice from the other side of the garden startled her. In the dim light, she could only make out a shadowy figure approaching the waterfall. She hadn't realized she was standing again, breathing heavily.

"Oh. I'm fine. It's okay." Her hands fluttered around her, arranging her sweater, checking her hair. "I was just going back to my room."

"Is that Ethel?"

"Yes. Who is that?

"It's Henry. Remember? We met on the road earlier."

"Oh, yes, Henry." He stood before her, in the usual khakis and a golf shirt.

"Well, I must seem a little strange," she said. "I'm feeling light-headed. Having some ... odd thoughts."

"That can happen in this place."

"Can it? Well, why does anyone put up with it? It seems dangerous. It's almost like I'm dreaming while I'm awake."

Henry laughed.

"What's so funny?"

"You saw Anandaji today didn't you?" He raised his moon-shaped eyebrows.

"Yes."

"Well, that can be quite moving."

"Moving? No. We just had tea."

"It can stir things up to be with a teacher. It's natural, a physical response to letting go of the mind a little. Once you get used to it, it can be interesting. You just have to get the fear out of it."

"What are you talking about? Everyone's crazy at this place!"

Henry laughed again. "Isn't it wonderful?"

"Not at all. Excuse me, but I think I've had enough of this. I'll be heading back in the morning. Very nice to meet you." Ethel fumbled on the bench beside her, seeking out her half-eaten cookie, not sure of what she was saying.

"Ethel. Don't. Maybe I can help sort it out."

"Thank you, but I have to leave. This is all wrong." Ethel's voice cracked, threatening tears. She hurried out of the garden toward her room.

Once there she went directly to her suitcase, opened it on the bed, and began gathering her things. She grabbed her pink sweatsuit from where it lay draped over a chair and yanked her cell-phone charger out of the outlet under the night table. She swiped her latex pillow from the bed, reached for her windbreaker in the closet, and located her makeup kit, still set open on the table. She checked through its contents: blush, mascara, powder, foundation, a collection of eye pencils and lipsticks. But something was missing: her favorite Dior lipstick that she'd just bought last week at Saks. Terra Rose, $24.50, no bargain, but the saleswoman had assured her it was the perfect shade for her coloring. She scanned the room, then knelt and searched under the bed, scrunching her nose at the musty carpet that scratched against her chin. "Feh, they don't clean this place."

A light sweat broke out on her face as she rushed to the bathroom to see if the lipstick had rolled into the trash below the sink. Nothing but floss strings and folded Kleenex dabbed with the impression of her lips tinted in Terra Rose. "Shit. Shit, shit, shit, shit." Ethel didn't usually swear, but this was worth it. Not just the lipstick, but the whole crazy affair.

Nine

IN ORDER FOR ETHEL to get to the parking lot from her room, she had to pass through the corridor to the lecture hall where satsang was just beginning. From the end of the empty hallway, she could see the woman from the main building reach to close the door inside the hall, her yellow-gray head tipping reverently downward, as if closing a door was a prayerful act. Boy, was she glad she was leaving. She was now in full tilt with her suitcase in tow, enjoying imagining the satsang beginning without her. But as she neared the doorway, a figure collided against her.

"Oh my!" Her suitcase crashed down beside her.

"I'm so sorry." Anandaji's voice echoed in her ear, followed by his gentle laughter. "Ethel, it's you."

Ethel stared at him, dumbfounded. He bent down to right her suitcase.

"Where did you come from?" She asked. "There was no one here!"

"Oh, just in there," he said, pointing to a door tucked around the corner from the lecture hall. "I'm a little late tonight. Enjoying another cup of Earl Grey." He smiled, his ocean eyes sparkling. "Ethel, are you leaving?"

"Well, yes. I thought I might." She fidgeted with the hem of her sweater.

"Might?"

"Well, no. I mean, yes, I'm leaving."

He was freshly dressed in his tunic. Ethel thought it was cute how he wore tunics only to satsang.

"That's too bad."

"Why?"

"Because it's nice to have you around."

Ethel raised her eyebrows. "Why?"

"You're fun." He shrugged.

"Fun? People don't usually refer to me as fun."

"Well you are for me." He smiled.

"And why's that?"

"Because you don't take things too seriously. Here, I mean. At the ashram. That's a good thing."

Ethel shrank inside remembering her last hour in the garden and packing up her room. If only he'd seen that! She looked at Anandaji, his eyes twinkling at her. She wished she didn't like him so much. She noticed that none of the distrust she felt earlier was there now. "I've been having some strange thoughts," she said.

"Thought can be tricky," he said. "Some are bad news. Better to dump them in the garbage if they're not doing you any good."

"These were that kind, I think."

"Were they about leaving?"

"Sort of."

"When it comes to spiritual things, it's good to follow your heart, not your thoughts. Thoughts can be scary and confusing, and they get you nowhere. What does your heart say?"

Spiritual things? Since when was she concerned with spiritual things? But something inside felt different. She noticed the soft amber weave of Anandaji's tunic. A space had cleared in her chest. She took a deep breath.

"Well, I'd better go in," Anandaji said. "I don't like to be late. Take care, Ethel."

Anandaji disappeared behind the door. She imagined him walking down the aisle toward his seat. She knew how it felt to be among those watching him. For the first time she realized she enjoyed knowing he was entering the room, the quiet he brought with him. She felt sad, missing it. Realizing there was this attraction to Anandaji frightened her, but it also intrigued her, and led her through the door just a few paces behind him, her suitcase still sitting in the corridor.

Anandaji began the satsang with questions from the group and Henry's was the first hand up. He strode to the mike. "Anandaji, this question has been with me for a while. I've been wondering about what it is that keeps me wanting to be with you. It's out of character for me to be following a teacher. I've always been independent. Can you explain why this happens?"

Ethel couldn't believe it. There was Henry, speaking her mind again.

Anandaji smiled warmly at Henry. "The teacher is your own heart, Henry. He's not separate from you. He's only a reminder of your true self. That's where the love and attraction come from."

"But we're not the same, Anandaji. There's something I think you can teach me. That's why I'm here."

"And what is that?" said Anandaji. "What can I teach you?"

Henry thought for a while. "You teach me how to be. How to be myself."

Anandaji laughed. "Yes, a self you already are. There'll come a time when you'll know this so thoroughly, you won't see a difference between us. You'll see that the real teacher has been you all along."

"But," blurted Ethel. Her hand shot up. Several heads whipped around to look at her.

"Yes, Ethel," Anandaji said, happily. "Come up!"

"Come up?" Ethel's hand was now plastered to her lap. What had she done?

"Yes, you have a question?"

"Can I ask it from here?"

"Well, yes, but people may not hear you."

The group laughed, and the woman next to Ethel nodded to her encouragingly. "It's not so bad," she whispered.

Ethel rose and excused herself through the five sets of legs in her row. She made her way up the aisle, wondering what she would say when she got to the mike. Her heart was in her throat. Henry smiled and stepped away from the mike.

"Anandaji," she said, startled by the boom of her voice throughout the room. "Hundreds of people think you're something special. You mean to tell me they're all coming here, paying good money for rooms and meals, just to find out that they could stay home and be their own teachers?"

The room broke into a roar and Anandaji shook with laughter. Ethel laughed along politely, but wasn't sure she got the joke.

"Ethel," said Anandaji. "Remember what I told you just now about listening to your heart? In our culture we listen to our minds. We worship thought. We think our thoughts and beliefs are who we actually are. We travel so far away from our authenticity, the simplicity of our beings, that sometimes we need a reminder, an example."

"And that's you? What makes you the example?"

"That's for you to judge, Ethel."

Ethel thought about this. Anandaji really wasn't asking anything of her. He was just sitting there, saying what he felt. She could take it or leave it, and something in her kept telling her to take it. "Anandaji, why don't I want to leave?"

"Because your heart is held here for now, Ethel. Your heart is being allowed to lead, for once. It's different, isn't it?"

Ten

THE NEXT MORNING ETHEL woke up early enough to attend the first meditation session and decided to give it a go. What the heck. There must be something to this sitting-around-doing-nothing stuff or else everyone wouldn't be so dead set on doing it.

She joined the crowd in the lobby outside the meditation hall, waiting for it to open at seven fifteen. She even looked the part with her blanket wrapped around her like a shawl and her latex pillow under her arm, hoping it would cushion her chair for the half hour of sitting.

As the doors opened, she spotted a nice aisle seat near the back. She got comfortable and watched the rest of the group trail in. There were Henry and Phil, there was the woman who had egged her onto the mike last night, and there, she couldn't quite believe it, was Debra.

Their eyes met and it seemed to Ethel that Debra's were teary. She rushed over and took the seat beside Ethel giving her a long, full hug.

"Hi Mom," she whispered softly. Silence was required in the hall. "I can't believe we're here together."

Before Ethel could answer, the meditation bell sounded from the front of the hall and Anandaji was at his station. He bowed before the group, then folded into a cross-legged position in his seat and closed his eyes.

Ethel looked at Debra. She, too, had closed her eyes. She was wearing the shawl Fred gave her for her birthday last May: half cashmere, half silk with beautiful embroidery at the edges. Periwinkle—Debra's favorite color. On her feet were the socks Casey had knit her at camp years ago, with happy stripes of turquoise, yellow, and pink. Her hands lay loosely in her lap, the wedding band and diamond so familiar to Ethel, the sight of them brought a wave of love. She remembered when Debra and Fred had chosen the rings and how happy Debra had been to find a band with some character, etched in filigree, and a diamond that lay flat and wouldn't catch on her sweaters. My practical daughter. Emotion caught in Ethel's throat. My daughter. Debra's hands were those of a fifty year old, reddened from housework and dry from neglect. She never used the hand cream Ethel gave her. But they were still delicate and thin, like they were when she was a girl.

Ethel took a deep breath and closed her eyes, thinking she should probably attempt some meditation, but it was hard to get her thoughts off of Debra. Why didn't she call to let her know she was coming? Maybe she had. Ethel didn't even check her messages last night. She was so tired after satsang. It felt wonderful to be sitting next to Debra now, feeling her so close. Her eyes popped back open. She examined Debra's soft halo of hair, wondering if she might have grown a little grayer since the last time she'd seen her. She refused to color. It struck Ethel as funny that she, at seventy-two, was a frosted blonde, while her daughter was almost completely gray. Debra, always the rebel, never afraid to ask those piercing questions, to set herself apart. Even before her teenage years, Debra was grilling the rabbi during Bible class, wanting to know who God was, and why he did such terrible things to the Egyptians, drowning them in the Red Sea while the Jews went free. And then, when she was well into her hippie phase, there was that time when Pop was visiting, and Debra asked him what God meant to him. Ethel only heard traces of their conversation. She was busy in the kitchen and they were slightly out of earshot in the living room, but now she could picture the scene: Debra in that crocheted poncho she always wore and her wild, frizzy ringlets, and Pop, with his soft blue-gray eyes and his hands wrapped securely around his prayer book.

They're the same! They're just the same, always asking those probing questions, always wanting to know more, always searching. Nothing like me, really. Ethel took in the gentle quiver of Debra's translucent eyelids, her slow, barely perceptible breath, her faint smile. It could be Pop praying. It really could. She looked over at Anandaji, then at the crowd, so peaceful and quiet, she could almost hear the silence. She looked again at Debra and marveled at how completely lost she was in her meditation. She seemed so at home in this place. Ethel hadn't known this part of her life. What she was like here. What she felt. She hadn't wanted to know. A wave of sadness came over her, even guilt. She flashed on the many conversations she'd had with Debra over the years, the skepticism and doubt she voiced over Debra's spiritual life. For the first time she felt regret. What was she thinking? Debra wasn't doing anything dangerous. She was just sitting here, relaxing. Or more than that, she was settling down. She was settling deep down. She thought of how hard Debra worked during the week and how money hadn't always been so easy to come by for her and Fred. Unlike Ethel, she'd had to work through all the years she'd raised her children, even when she would have enjoyed staying home with them. She felt happy for Debra now, which surprised her. It was so out of the ordinary. But there it was. Though something inside still struggled with the idea of Debra's love for the ashram, something in her also understood it. Relief shone from Debra's face, and Ethel enjoyed the thought that she might have something to do with it.

Debra took a strong breath in, shuddering a little on her exhale and for a brief moment she seemed almost mysterious to Ethel. Where had she come from? Out of nowhere, it seemed, she just dropped into Ethel's life this morning. Debra: the child she'd fed and raised, the person she counted as more important than any other in her life; Debra, with Milt's round chin and those long, slender fingers as familiar as her own; Debra, with her deep, probing mind. Though this was the daughter she knew with every ounce of her being, she suddenly seemed such a miracle. Ethel couldn't believe she even existed. The sensation was not unlike what she'd felt fifty years earlier when she'd first held her as a newborn, the utter impossibility of it, the shock and exhilaration of birthing a fully formed human being. Ethel thought of that moment with Anandaji and his prodding her about the chickadee. She understood now that she might not actually know what a bird was. Looking at Debra beside her she wondered if she could ever really know who she was either. This person she called daughter.

Eleven

AFTER THE MEDITATION, ANANDAJI welcomed the newcomers who had arrived that morning for a three-day weekend retreat. The crowd was larger and people sat on pillows along the walls. Anandaji asked that those who had been there all week allow the weekend visitors to have a chance to speak. As soon as he nodded for questions to begin, Debra's hand shot up. In a flash she was at the mike.

"Hi, Anandaji."

"Hi. It's Debra, right? Welcome."

"Thank you. I've wanted to ask you this question for a while and have held back for fear of sounding silly, but I'm just going to go ahead and ask it."

Ethel was enthralled watching Debra at the mike. She was so comfortable with Anandaji, as if they were the only two people in the room.

"Sounding silly is a good thing," Anandaji said, "It's taking a risk. Go for it."

"Well, since I was little, I've always wanted to know what God was. And since I've been coming to see you, I think I have a clearer sense of it, but you rarely use the word God. You talk about consciousness and oneness and truth, but not God. I wondered if you could do that for me. Talk about God a little."

"Well sure." Anandaji crossed his legs. Ethel noticed he was wearing sweat socks. "But first I want to tell you why I'm reluctant to use the word."

"Yes," said Debra. "I'd like to know that."

"The word God can be overused and carries a lot of different connotations. You never know for sure what people mean by it. I like using words that express the abstract more simply: awareness, being, the absolute. If I had to choose one word to stand in for God, I'd pick reality. To me, reality says it all: simply what is here.

You, me, the whole shebang. There is no way to get out of God, because God is all there is."

"But how can we experience God more? How can we truly know God in everything we do?" Debra held her hands out, the way she always did when she asked a question, but there was more intensity to it than usual.

"Well, in truth, you already are, just by simply being. God is the most obvious thing there is because it's all there is. God is right in front of your nose, though most of us don't notice it." He smiled and pointed at Debra. "God is your nose!"

Everyone laughed. Ethel looked at Debra, who flushed with happiness the way she did when she'd had a glass of wine at family gatherings.

"Being with God is the simplest thing in the world," Anandaji told her. "The least common denominator. Stop feeling like you have to do anything. Stop trying. Just be. Amazing things will happen."

"Yes," Debra nodded. "The times I've done that have been incredible. There's no doing in it. It doesn't feel like anything is up to me. It just feels like I'm being the natural movement of myself through time. But I wish it happened more often."

"Yes, there's the rub," said Anandaji. "That desire for more. That grasping. That's what you can look at now."

Anandaji took a sip of water while he looked at Debra. "God includes the ordinary times when you feel like nothing is happening. It includes not only the bliss but the disappearance of it too."

Debra was quiet, pondering Anandaji's words. Ethel was totally confused. What were they talking about? Why was this always happening? Just when she thought she might be understanding what was going on at this place, something happened to convince her she didn't. And it would have been one thing if just anybody were asking these questions, but it was Debra. Her Debra. The Debra she sent to Hebrew school for twelve years. The Debra who sang the prayers so sweetly at her bat mitzvah and made Pop beam with pride. "Kvelling," he called it. Kvelling for his little madala. This Debra was asking crazy questions about God. And who was she asking? A guru with a shaved head and a nutty name. That's who. Ethel was getting that gotta-get-out-of-here feeling again, but she wasn't listening to it. She was staying put. She had to hear where this thing ended up. She had to be there for Debra if it didn't end up well. She had to be there, to set her straight.

Finally, Debra said, "It's hard to accept the unhappy times as God too."

"What is an unhappy time?"

Ethel almost laughed out loud. An unhappy time is an unhappy time, for God's sake. What else would it be? He's always with the riddles. She looked around to see if anyone else found this funny, but all she saw was a sea of thoughtful faces.

"You mean, what's the story that's making it unhappy?" asked Debra.

"Yes. Without the judgment that says something should not be happening, it could be quite a different thing. A traffic jam, say, without the resistance. Without the story that says it's wrong, it's annoying, and needs to go away, a traffic jam could be a fascinating event. Full of energy, color, and sounds."

"That's God too," Debra said.

"Yes."

God? thought Ethel. God is a traffic jam?

"Thank you," said Debra.

"My pleasure."

That's all? That's it? End of story? God's a traffic jam and thank you? Debra was still at the mike, smiling. Why didn't she sit down?

And then, Debra did something that almost brought Ethel to her feet. She bowed. Not a deep bow, just one of those little bows like Anandaji made before he sat down—a nod with her hands pressed together in front of her. But it was still a bow. Warmth rushed into Ethel's face. Her eyes bore into Debra as she walked back to her seat. When Debra smiled at her, she turned away.

Ethel sat stiffly through the rest of satsang, barely listening to the remaining questions, looking down at her hands. She felt like stone. Debra's warm body next to hers conjured none of the affection it had a half hour earlier during the group meditation. When satsang ended, Debra glanced at her and Ethel could see a flash of fear dart across her face as she took in Ethel's cold expression. Once outside she pulled Ethel aside.

"Mom, what's wrong? What happened?" People filed past them.

"What do you mean, what happened? My daughter bowed to a guru, that's what happened. My daughter asked a guru what God is, as if you never went to Hebrew school, as if we never taught you anything." Two women passing by smiled at each other. Ethel wondered if they'd overheard.

"Oh Mom." Debra shook her head. "I guess I should have known." She rolled her eyes.

"Don't roll your eyes at me, young lady."

"Young lady? Mom, c'mon. Listen to yourself. This is crazy."

"Me? I'm crazy? Did you hear yourself up there? Calling a traffic jam God? And what was that stuff about being movement in time, whatever you said. What are you talking about, Debra? You know better than this. You're a sensible girl. You're a nice, sensible girl." Ethel's voice cracked and tears flowed in, surprising her. She fought them back, but they insisted and she began searching in her coat pockets for a Kleenex.

"Here, Mom," said Debra, handing her a little pack of travel tissues.

Ethel smiled weakly and accepted the pack.

"Sensible Debra remembered her Kleenex."

Ethel laughed, but didn't answer. The tears had taken over and she gave way to the confusion and frustration that had been with her all week. It felt good, and when Debra put her arms around her, she ignored the impulse to push her away, to punish her. Instead she relaxed into the attention and comfort—the steady stroke of Debra's hand across her back, Debra's soft hair against her cheek. It felt as though Ethel was the daughter and Debra was the mother. Debra's chest was slight and strong against her own wider, softer frame. Ethel finally pulled away to blow her nose. Face to face, she was forced to see the warmth inside Debra's deep brown eyes.

"Why are you looking at me that way?" Ethel choked. "I wasn't very nice."

"Because I love you. And I understand how it can get here. I don't know what I'm feeling half the time. It's like quickly changing weather."

"You mean, this happens to you too?"

"It happens to everybody."

"Hmm, I think Henry tried to tell me something like that." Ethel blew her nose, hard, and dabbed her tears. "Why do you come then? I thought this was all about resting and getting calm. All that meditating and talking about God."

Debra laughed. "Yeah, it's about that too. But when you're serious, when you genuinely want to know yourself, you hit some rocky roads. You start seeing what's getting in the way of the truth."

Ethel stared at her. "This truth you're always after. I don't get it. I'm tired of hearing about it."

"I get tired of it sometimes too."

Ethel looked down at the Kleenex pack pressed between her fingers. "Your father always had a Kleenex pack, you know. He always had one in his coat pocket, wherever he went."

"I know. That must be where I got it from."

"I'd bring one of these to a funeral, but your father wouldn't go to a supermarket without one." She burst out laughing and Debra joined her, making the little ticking noise she did when she laughed hard. Ethel laughed even harder and worried she'd pee in her pants. But she didn't care. It felt so good to be laughing with Debra. Who else would understand how funny Milt was with his Kleenex pack? But that wasn't all she was laughing about. It was everything. It was the fact that Ethel was even in this place with statues of the Buddha everywhere she looked. It was the trail of baby boomers on their way to a lunch of veggie burgers and soy-milk shakes. It was Anandaji, and his impossible teachings, his Sol-like smile, and the fact that Ethel actually cared about him. It was Ethel's dripping mascara and Debra's lovely brown eyes that were tearing now from so much laughing, tearing so freely that Ethel took a Kleenex from the pack and bent toward her with it, to wipe her eyes.

Twelve

Ethel woke up early the next morning at six fifteen instead of the usual seven, fresh and excited to spend the day with Debra. It's not like they'd actually have anything to do around this place, but it would be fun just to be together. She laughed, thinking of how Anandaji liked to tell people just to be. Just be, he was fond of saying. Just be, rather than do.

After a quick shower, she rushed off to breakfast, hoping she'd find Debra there and sure enough, she spotted her at one of the silent tables near the back of the hall. Humph, why'd she choose silence? Wasn't she hoping to sit and chat with her mother?

Ethel walked right over with her tray of natural cornflakes, coffee and sliced fruit. "Debra," she whispered loudly. "Don't you want to sit together?"

Several people looked up from their breakfasts to stare at her, bemused more than annoyed. Debra flinched and shook her head, then mouthed, "Mom," as if in reprimand. Grabbing her tea and a dense-looking blueberry muffin, Debra motioned to Ethel to follow her to a small talking table where they could have privacy. Their chairs scraped as they sat down. Ethel scooted hers closer to Debra.

"Mom, it's rude to whisper like that."

"Rude? I thought it was polite to whisper. I was trying not to disturb anyone."

"It's a silent table, not a whispering table."

"Oh. Well, I'm sorry. But I think people get a little uptight here about those things, if you know what I mean. Too many sacred rules for my taste. And why were you in silence, anyway? Didn't you think I'd be coming?"

"Well, no actually. I didn't think you'd be up so early. And I wasn't in the mood to talk anyway. I like the morning solitude when I'm here."

"I'm sorry to disturb you."

"You're not disturbing me. I just felt like being quiet. I didn't feel like hearing myself talk. I didn't wake up in the greatest mood."

"What's wrong?"

"Nothing."

"I can tell there's something wrong."

"I don't want to talk. That's why I was in silence."

"Silence, shmilence. It's good to get things off your chest."

Debra sighed. "I'm not sure that's always true, Mom. Sometimes it's better to just watch your thinking and not take it seriously."

Ethel looked at Debra a while. "You seem tired, dear. Is everything okay at home? Why didn't Fred come?"

"Everything's fine, Mom. Fred had to work. He's hoping for that promotion, remember?"

"Oh, yeah. How are the kids?"

"Fine. They're both fine." Debra sounded exasperated.

"Debra, what is it?" Ethel's voice raised, imploring.

"It's not something you'd understand." She ran her fingers through her hair.

"Try me."

"It's a spiritual thing."

"Well, I'm here, aren't I?" Ethel put her arms out and smiled.

"Yes, you are, and I can't quite believe it, actually. How was it with Anandaji, anyway? You haven't told me." Debra took a sip of tea and broke off a piece of muffin.

"It was very nice, very nice. Very normal. But also, not normal. You want a strawberry?"

"No, thanks. That's a good way of putting it, Mom. Normal and not normal."

"He reminds me of Sol."

"Sol? Oh, c'mon Mom. Anandaji's nothing like Sol."

"The smile."

Debra shrugged. "I still can't believe you're here."

"Why is it so unbelievable?"

"Because you've always given me a hard time about the ashram. It's not like you've been understanding, you know."

"I guess I haven't." Ethel felt a wave of guilt.

"That hasn't been exactly easy on me." Debra peered at her under raised eyebrows.

"Yes," Ethel said. "Yes, I can see how you'd feel that way." She wanted to say more, but found it hard to. She knew what Debra wanted. She wanted Ethel to approve of the ashram, and she wasn't quite ready to. "Debra, I can see there's no real harm here, but I'm not sure it's necessarily a good thing, either. I think it could become a habit, a dependency, if you know what I mean. There are people here that seem like they may be addicted to the place. I think you have to watch out for that."

"Do you really think I have to watch out for that, Mom? Do you think I'm in danger of becoming addicted? I work all week. I take care of the kids and Fred. I volunteer at hospice, I sit on the school board, for God's sake. Do you really think I'd pack up and move to the ashram?"

"It was worth a little warning."

"No it wasn't."

"You're a little testy this morning, dear."

"I'm ... ugh. I should have just stayed in silence."

Ethel moved an apple slice around on her plate and said nothing.

"I'm feeling ... I feel like I'll never get there," said Debra.

Ethel looked at her, alert to the confidentiality in her tone. "Where, dear? Where won't you get?"

"Enlightened. I'll never get enlightened. My mind is too busy."

Ethel laughed out loud.

"Thanks a lot, Mom. That's very understanding."

"Well, I just can't believe that's what you're upset about."

Debra chewed her muffin slowly.

"Enlightened," said Ethel. "Everyone here wants to be enlightened." She shook her head. "You know, Debra. Anandaji himself says not to make enlightenment a goal."

Debra looked at Ethel. "Boy, you've been listening. I never thought I'd hear my mother say that."

Ethel laughed. "It makes sense, though. If enlightenment is a state of perfect contentment, it would be pretty silly to beat yourself up to get there."

"Wow, Mom, that's pretty good."

"Besides," said Ethel, encouraged. "You're just fine the way you are. At least I think so."

Debra's face softened, and some strain fell away.

"You are, sweetheart. You're a wonderful, wonderful girl. You don't need to change. I can't imagine this enlightenment could make you any more wonderful than you already are." Ethel patted Debra's hand.

"Thanks, Mom," said Debra. She pulled a Kleenex from the pack in her pocket and blew her nose.

"And what's wrong with a busy mind? Doesn't everyone's mind get busy sometimes? It's normal. It's normal to have a busy mind."

Debra shrugged, unconvinced.

"Just be happy you're not like Aunt Frieda. Her mind's so busy it pours right out through her mouth. It's gotten so bad I'm afraid to call her. It's impossible to get off the phone."

Debra laughed, but not as hard as she normally would over an Aunt Frieda joke. She shook her head as if to clear it. "I'm so sick of thinking!" she moaned.

"Debra, what could be more human than thinking? For God's sake, you're human!"

"Anandaji's human too and he doesn't have a head full of thoughts all day."

"How do you know?"

"Trust me, Ma. He doesn't."

Ethel thought about this. Anandaji did seem calm. It was hard to imagine him fretting over anything. But thoughts? He probably had plenty.

"He has thoughts," Ethel said definitively. "He just doesn't mind them."

"That's true," Debra said slowly, looking at Ethel in amazement. "That's what I can't seem to do. Stop minding that I'm thinking so much. Stop minding that I'm not enlightened."

"This is getting crazy, Debra. You're talking in circles. Why don't you just relax?"

"I can't!" Debra's voice rose, drawing attention. One very peaceful but serious-looking fellow sitting near them got up to find a table further away. Debra took a few bites of muffin. "This muffin's dry," she said.

"They don't use eggs," said Ethel. "Whoever heard of a muffin without eggs." Debra laughed.

"You know," Ethel went on. "When I met with Anandaji I asked him if he really had anything so magical to teach anybody, and he said no, that he's no different than anybody else and everyone has what he has inside them."

"I've heard him say that."

"Do you think he's lying?"

"No, not lying—of course not. But I don't think he means we're the same when it comes to the amount of baggage we carry around. Just our essential nature."

"What do you mean? What's this essential nature? I don't get that part."

"I'm not sure I can describe it. It's what we are without our attachments and hang-ups, when we're free from our conditioning and karma."

"Karma?"

"That's even harder to explain."

"Why is conditioning so bad? Or even hang-ups? Those are the things that make us interesting. Everybody's a little quirky. Even Anandaji. I bet if you got to know him better, as well as you know Fred, or me, you'd see plenty of baggage."

"I don't know, Mom. Yeah, probably. Maybe." Debra pulled on the hem of her olive-colored T-shirt. "I'm getting tired of this whole thing."

"So, give it up. Why are you knocking yourself out with this stuff? Don't come to the ashram. Just go on with your life. You don't need this."

Debra broke into tears.

"Debra, honey, what is it?" Ethel looked at Debra, confused. "Sweetheart." She leaned over and hugged her. Debra smiled and blew her nose.

"I'm just emotional. I've been at this for over thirty years, meditating twice a day, reading every spiritual book I can get my hands on, and what do I have to show for it?"

"Actually," Ethel said slowly, considering whether to say what she was thinking, "plenty, you have plenty."

Debra squinted at her.

"There's something to be said for all this," said Ethel.

"Yes?" said Debra.

"You're more peaceful, or something. Something's different than it used to be."

"Like what?"

"I'm not sure I can put my finger on it." Ethel was a little uncertain of whether to go on. She didn't want to encourage Debra too much. She was likely to go all haywire over the ashram like some of the people here—that woman from the main building who seemed to have no life outside this place. Ethel didn't want that for Debra. But she couldn't hide what she was thinking and she knew it would make Debra happy.

"Well, I don't know," she finally said, "I guess this could have happened anyway, with aging. People get wiser and kinder as they age. Sometimes."

She looked down at her wilting cornflakes and stirred them around in the bowl.

"Do you mean I'm wiser and kinder than I used to be?"

"Yes. And more patient too. You don't jump on me as much."

"And you think that may be due to spiritual practice?"

"Yes. I can see how it would be. I didn't used to, but now I do."

"Thank you, Mom. That's nice to hear. You've never said anything like that before."

"I mean it, dear. Maybe you're already enlightened," said Ethel. She pushed the cornflakes aside and took a sip of coffee.

"Yeah, right." Debra crumbled the muffin between her fingers.

"You could do with a few less spiritual books, though. The last time I was at your house every shelf was covered with them. What happened to all the nice novels you used to read?"

"I'm not sure. For some reason they don't interest me anymore." She wiped a few crumbs off the table.

"You know what you need to do, sweetheart? You need to let yourself be who you are, with all the hang-ups, all the kaarma." She drew out the word, trying it out in her vocabulary.

Debra lifted her head. Her eyes were dry and wide open.

"Say that again, Mom."

"You need to let yourself be, dear. Just let yourself be." Ethel met Debra's gaze and felt a tingle in her chest. The last time she looked this grateful was when Ethel nursed her through the flu. She'd spent days spoon feeding her chicken soup and dabbing her face with a cold washcloth, carting the kids to school and soccer and fixing dinner for them and Fred. Debra's fevered eyes had fixed on Ethel with the biggest thank you she'd ever seen. There it was again.

Thirteen

ETHEL WAS SLEEPY DURING morning satsang, wishing she was back in bed, making up for that lost hour of sleep. Or better yet, back at home in her queen-size bed where she could spread out properly. She hadn't slept in a single bed in years, and she was tired of it. Her feet always hung over one side, the pillows were forever dropping off into the slat between the edge of the bed and the wall, and the bed kept rolling further away from the wall whenever she rolled over. Looking around the room, she half-listened to Anandaji go on about the same stuff he always did—how realizing our essential nature was only a breath away, how we were all one, and how each person was her own best teacher. She was feeling more and more that she was pretty much done with the ashram. She had gained all she was going to get from it. If she was her own best teacher, she might as well leave. She'd thought so all along. She glanced at Anandaji as one would at a picture of a long-ago friend—with affection, but waning interest. She'd head out when Debra did the next day. That would only make sense. She looked over at Debra who was listening raptly to Anandaji with no trace of her early morning despair detectable on her face. Ethel leaned toward her until her lips were almost touching Debra's ear.

"I might as well leave when you do tomorrow," she whispered.

Debra jerked up in her seat.

"Mom," she whispered sharply. "Please don't talk during satsang."

Ethel pulled away, annoyed with the reprimand. She squirmed in her seat and checked her watch. Satsang could easily go another half hour or even forty-five minutes since Anandaji seemed to enjoy going overtime. She considered whether to sneak out of the hall. Debra would be annoyed. Well, so what, she was annoyed with her anyway. Ethel looked down at her nails. She hadn't touched them up all week and the edges were starting to peel. Didn't matter much here. She'd only seen one person so far wearing polish—an awful neon blue color on the square edged nails of a young college girl with a tattoo of a wreath of flowers around her arm, plenty of makeup, and more earrings than Ethel could imagine fitting on one ear. Two were a flurry of feathers hanging down along her neck. Ethel looked around the room to see if she could find this girl now and was surprised to see her walking to the mike, her shock of pink hair standing on edge and her blue nails glittering on the ends of her fingers. She was also, Ethel realized, crying, but out of excitement or joy, rather than sadness.

"Anandaji," she said, her crisp voice ringing around the room. "I feel like I've been reborn. I don't know how to describe it."

Oy, another one of these, thought Ethel.

"I mean, everything looks so alive. There's so much peace everywhere. Inside and out." She spread her arms wide to indicate the whole room. "The only problem is, I love life so much, I'm even more afraid to die."

"Who dies?" asked Anandaji.

The girl just looked at him.

"Investigating death can be a powerful practice," said Anandaji. "Ask yourself who it is that is loving life right now, and who it is that would leave it were you to die. What would you lose and who would do the losing?"

The girl was still. "My body would be gone," she said, "my senses, my ability to feel this peace."

"Who is feeling this?" asked Anandaji.

"I am."

"And who is this I?"

What crazy questions. Always the crazy questions. Who dies. Who is this I. What does he think we are, aliens? Ethel shook her head, thinking how nice it would be to be around people who talked about normal things for a change. She'd be sure to call Fran as soon as she got home.

"Who feels this peace?" asked Anandaji again.

"Itself," the girl said slowly, as if tasting the word. "It seems like the peace is felt by some part of itself. Or the peace is just there, just me, just what I am."

Anandaji nodded and smiled. "Does this die? Can this die?" He held out an open palm.

"I don't know," said the girl. "I'm not sure."

Anandaji waited for her.

The next time she spoke her voice was a little shaky. "I'm afraid that the peace doesn't last. I'd like to think it does, but maybe it passes like everything else. Maybe I'm making it up. Underneath, what's left when the peace isn't there feels empty and dark. That's what I'm afraid of."

The girl was trembling a little and Ethel was worried about her. She wondered how smart it was to be talking about death. What's the use of that? What a morbid topic. She liked it better when the girl was focusing on her peaceful feelings; even though Ethel wasn't sure she bought all that stuff about loving life so much. Life is nice, but let's face it—it's no bowl of cherries.

Ethel looked over at Debra and tried to catch her eye to see what she thought about all this, but Debra was riveted to Anandaji.

"It's okay," he was saying. "Just let it be there. It's just fear. It just needs to be seen."

The girl's painted eyelids closed, her body quivered, making her feathery earrings sway. People around the hall sat with their eyes closed or watching the scene with compassionate looks on their faces. She caught sight of Henry; his head was bowed as if he was praying.

Ethel heard a soft sob next to her. It was Debra. She reached out to comfort her, but Debra put a hand out to stop her. Not annoyed like before, just a gesture that said: It's okay, Mom. I'm all right.

Why was Debra crying? Was she worried for the girl? Maybe they were friends. Or … maybe she was remembering Milt. Milt in their old king-size bed, wasting away during those last days of the cancer. His yellow skin, so little left of him, as tiny as a child, his breathing labored and uneven. The hospice nurse arrived, and Ethel was crying so hard she had to go to the guest room for a while, leaving Debra and the nurse to sit with him. While she was gone—it couldn't have been more than a half hour—he died. That was what Debra was remembering now. Ethel was sure of it. She'd always felt guilty she hadn't been there, not just for Milt but for Debra. They could have shared the memory of Milt drifting away, as horrible as it was. Now she wanted to pull Debra from her seat and bring her outside. What good was this? What good was dwelling on such things?

The girl wiped her eyes, sweeping shiny dots of blue across her face. "The fear passed. There's just quietness now." She took a breath, shuddering like a child finishing up a good cry. "Peace," she said. "It always seems to come back to that."

"It does, doesn't it?" Anandaji answered.

"Is that what death is?"

"Who knows?" Anandaji's eyes widened. He smiled at her.

"Oh, you," the girl giggled and bowed her head, preparing to leave.

"No, really," said Anandaji. "Who knows?"

The girl thought for a while. "No one," she said. "No one knows anything." She laughed.

"What does that feel like, to be no one who knows nothing?"

A gentle wave of laughter passed over the room. The girl thought again, her cherry lips pinched in concentration.

"It feels good," she said finally. "It feels empty … in an interesting way. Open, with a little fear in it—sort of, bottomless. But it's okay."

"Yes," said Anandaji. "Hang out there a while. See what it feels like to be bottomless."

The girl held her hands together and touched her chin; her dark fingernails lined up in a row. She bounced back to her seat.

Ethel's mouth hung open. She stared at Anandaji, not knowing what to make of this lesson. What was he trying to tell the girl and the group? She looked at Debra, who was smiling contentedly, wiping tears away and nodding to herself. Ethel looked over at Henry. His face was turned intently toward Anandaji, his eyes were filled with gratitude. She thought of Milt, his thin, yellow face, his shrunken shoulders. He had looked so much smaller when she returned to the room and found him with Debra, sobbing by his side.

Fourteen

Everyone remained seated after satsang while Anandaji left the hall. This annoyed Ethel more than usual. *As if he's a king or something.* She would have liked to express this to somebody, but she knew Debra wouldn't want to hear anything negative about Anandaji. The thought simmered inside her. She waited restlessly for the door to close behind him, the signal for the rest of the group to file out of the hall toward lunch. Debra walked in silence beside Ethel to the dining hall, lost in herself.

When they got to the lunch line, she told Ethel she was going for the bag-lunch option.

"I want to eat alone by the lake," she said. Ethel looked at her, trying to hide her disappointment and hurt.

"Mom," Debra said, placing a hand on Ethel's shoulder, "this has nothing to do with you. It's what I like to do when I'm here. I work all week. I need the rest. You and I will have plenty of time to catch up when we get home."

"What do they put in those bag lunches?"

"Oh, nothing special. Usually tofu salad or peanut butter and jelly and a piece of fruit. Sometimes a dessert."

"Those date bar things?"

"Something like that."

"Okay dear, have a restful time," Ethel said halfheartedly. She figured Debra needed to think more about Milt. She wished she'd invited her along.

"Thanks, Mom." Ethel watched Debra place herself in line at the bag lunch window. She noticed how well Debra blended in with the others: middle-aged, graying, and dressed in loose cotton clothes. Ethel thought back to how she dressed when she was fifty: shirtwaist dresses and beehive hairdos, nylon stockings and heels. They were so different. She wondered if they'd even be friends if they were the same age. Ethel couldn't imagine choosing to eat alone by the lake. Her mind was jittery with thoughts about the satsang.

"Hi, Ethel. How are you this fine day?"

Ethel turned. Henry hovered behind her in line, his gentle eyes brimming with an affection that didn't seem exclusively for her, but for everything and everyone. He was so relaxed and happy all the time, as if life was just rolling along. Nothing seemed to trouble him.

"Oh, okay," said Ethel. "But I wasn't too pleased with that last talk. What did you think of it?"

"I was very moved." Henry's voice caught in his throat.

"What was so moving about it?"

"I think I told you I lost my wife last year."

"Yes. Yes. I'm sorry," said Ethel, "my condolences." She moved a few paces ahead, standing sideways in line so she could face Henry.

"Thank you," he said. "It hasn't always been easy. But Anandaji's teachings, like the things he said this morning, have been very helpful to me."

"How?"

"They stop me in my tracks. They help me rethink my attitude about what happened."

"What do you mean?" asked Ethel.

"Well naturally I'd rather have my wife back, but Anandaji has helped me accept that she's not here, and to face the fact that I'm not in charge; life is." He smoothed his hands over the wisps of hair on his head. "He's even helped me see that my wife wasn't necessarily my wife. I know that sounds crazy. What I mean is that none of us are who we appear to be. We're all just playing our parts, for as long as we're allowed to."

Ethel gazed at a tall, bearded man further back in line. She tried to understand. How could Milt be anybody other than Milt?

"I lost my husband too," she said.

"I'm sorry," Henry said. They collected their plates and silverware.

Ethel nodded.

"It's been some time. But it doesn't always feel like it." She scooped a burrito from a serving tray and motioned to an empty table. "Would you like to join me?"

"I'd love to. Do you want to sit outside? It's beautiful."

Ethel headed to the outdoor tables while Henry collected their drinks and chips and salsa. She found a small picnic table in the shade of some pines where they could sit alone. He's a nice man, she thought, a little too much with this ashram business, but nice. Milt would be so surprised to find her here. What on earth are you thinking Ethel? She imagined him asking her, a teasing smile on his round, jovial face. She loved how his eyelids slanted downward, giving him a thoughtful, knowing expression, as if he knew her better than she knew herself. And he sometimes did. He knew her better than anyone. A wave of missing him passed through her. Suddenly she felt very alone.

"Apple juice okay?" Henry placed a chilled glass and a bowl of chips in front of her.

"What? Oh, yes, thank you. That's fine. Henry?" Ethel asked a bit tentatively, "what do you do with the missing feeling?"

Henry folded and smoothed out a paper napkin with his long fingers. "I just feel it," he said.

"Well, of course. But is that all? I mean, haven't you learned any tricks from Anandaji? It sounds like he's helped you a lot."

"That is the trick, feeling it." He scooped some salsa onto a chip.

"But that's so obvious."

"Not to everyone. Most of the time we try to push it away, try to ward it off. We don't want to look grief in the face. I mean, really look at it. Not just the surface of it, but all the way through." He popped a chip in his mouth.

"That sounds unhealthy," said Ethel. "If I think about my grief, I wind up feeling terrible. Horrible memories come." She looked down and brushed the bottom of her shoe over the scattered pine needles. "It was cancer. It wasn't pretty. Why should I feel that?"

"There's a fine line between allowing a feeling to play itself out and milking it. Giving it time to express itself is important; you can't suppress it."

He bit into his burrito.

"Have I been suppressing?" She meant to say this to herself, but she'd spoken the words out loud.

"Well, I don't know." Henry raised his crescent-moon eyebrows. "Only you would know that. But it's natural to do it. I mean, sad feelings are uncomfortable. But I'm learning they're not always what they feel like."

He wiped his mouth with a napkin, leaving some salsa behind.

"What do you mean?" Ethel wondered how sadness could feel like anything but sadness.

"Well, what are you feeling right now?" asked Henry.

"Confused. And I've been thinking about Milt, so I'm a little sad."

"Are you pushing the sadness away while we talk?"

Ethel thought. Was she trying not to feel the heaviness in her chest, trying not to see Milt's kind eyes?

"I guess so," she said quietly.

"What would happen if you just felt it?" Henry's voice softened to almost a whisper.

"You mean here? With you? With all these people around?"

She looked at the picnic table closest to them crammed with people. All this time Ethel had been holding a chip between her fingers. She hadn't eaten a thing. Now she bit firmly into the chip.

Henry took another bite of his burrito.

"Retreat is just the place for that sort of thing. People here understand. I don't mean to pry, though. Whatever you're comfortable with."

Ethel chewed on her chip and ate another, scooping the salsa methodically, while Henry rubbed his funny round nose.

"Okay," she said. "I'll feel it. It's there, anyway. It doesn't seem to be going anywhere."

Henry nodded. "Maybe it's hanging around until you give it some attention."

These were strange words, strange ways to look at this sadness she'd known for so long.

"What do you mean? You make it sound like a feeling has a life of its own, like it's separate from me."

"Well, what does it feel like?"

"I miss him." Ethel looked down at the uneaten burrito on her plate. "It's like stone, concrete, something hard inside."

"I know," said Henry.

He waited, not eating. Ethel closed her eyes and felt the hardness inside. After a while she realized it wasn't so hard anymore. It was changing, spreading out, softening. It wasn't so much about Milt. Or, maybe it was about him, but not about missing him. What had felt like a stone was more like a blanket of sadness. And the sadness wasn't even so sad; it was sort of sweet and melancholy. She actually liked it.

"It's different," she said, "I don't mind it so much anymore. It feels nice, like … love." She looked up, astonished.

"Beautiful," said Henry.

"Is this what Anandaji taught you?"

"Yes."

"Is this what you were feeling in the lecture hall? What Debra was feeling? And that girl at the mike?"

"I can't speak for the others," said Henry, "but I was feeling good, open, willing to feel whatever came down the pike."

"I see," said Ethel. "I think I get it."

She lowered her eyes, and lingered a few more minutes on the feelings inside. the sadness that turned into melancholy, and then into love. It was fading now and she found herself wishing it wouldn't go away.

Fifteen

AFTER LUNCH, ETHEL DECIDED to take a look around the bookstore, which was really more like a hippie gift shop. She'd visited the place several times already, but only to treat herself to those chocolate mint patties they had and to sample some exotic foot cream. She'd long since given up on actually buying a book. Each title was more incomprehensible than the next: *Uncovering the Now, Only This, Nothing Doing, You are Not.* As if that wasn't enough, many of the authors had convoluted Eastern names that made her brain hurt when she tried to pronounce them. A few books were by a certain rabbi who at first drew her attention, but when she inspected his picture on the jacket flap he looked so ridiculously happy that Ethel wondered if he'd lost his senses.

Several women were sorting through the racks of gauzy drawstring pants and endless shawls and wraps. Over in the corner a man slid his feet in and out of those funny foot-massage sandals with bumps on the insoles. Who could ever wear those? Like walking on pebbles! Across the aisle, the young woman with the painted blue nails was sampling the chanting CDs, her eyelids, shimmering green, were lightly closed, her feathery earrings swaying. Ethel took in the collective aromas of incense, soap, oils, and candles. She pinched the batting of a few meditation cushions, imagining what they'd be like to sit on. She even considered purchasing one for using on top of her chair in the lecture hall. What for? She was leaving tomorrow. Did she actually think she'd ever come back to the ashram? She stuffed the pillow back onto the shelf and wondered at herself. Why would she come back? Looking around the store at the sea of calm faces, everyone seeming as though they'd just had a massage, she felt the familiar longing for home.

After slathering her feet with cream that smelled like spiced oranges and made them tingle, she indulged in three mint patties. Then she decided to give the rabbi's books another try. She opened one in the middle.

Sh'ma yisrael, adonai elohenu, adonai echad, Hear oh Israel, the Lord our God, the Lord is One, was written across the top of the page, a prayer as familiar to Ethel as her own name. This was the watchword of the Jewish faith, the first prayer Pop had taught her, and Milt had taught Debra, the prayer Milt had mouthed on his deathbed, and the prayer Debra was always insisting said the exact same thing as the Buddhists. Something Ethel still didn't understand.

Ethel read on. She wasn't surprised to find the rabbi's language was much like Anandaji's. *The Lord is One doesn't mean there is only one God as opposed to many gods, as many people think,* she read. *It means everything is God and everything is One because that's all there is.*

Ethel held her place and flipped to the jacket flap to study the rabbi's picture again. He wore a hand-crocheted yarmulke. His prayer shawl was striped in every color of the rainbow, rather than the usual blue. Pop would think he's meshuggener, but his eyes had a welcoming look about them and his smile seemed more genuine than the first time she'd glanced at it. Rabbi Simon L'Chaim, the caption read, invites Jews and seekers everywhere to find

God vibrating, not only inside our most ancient prayers, but in every ordinary moment of life.

"A Jewish Anandaji," chuckled Ethel. She turned back to the Sh'ma page.

Rabbi L'Chaim urged: *Look at the trees and birds, the houses, cars, street signs, and roads. Look at your loved ones. Look at your hands and feet and feel your breath flowing in and out. How did all this get here? What miracle sustains it? What presence allows it? That presence is God. It's all God.* Don't forget traffic jams, thought Ethel. Traffic jams are God. She didn't think Rabbi L'Chaim could explain this to her any better than Anandaji. She thumbed through a few more pages, then gazed around the bookstore filling up with people looking for something to do before afternoon satsang.

"He's a great teacher," she heard someone say.

She looked up. The feathery earring girl was smiling down at her with her bright red lips.

"Is he?" said Ethel. "How so?"

"He's the coolest rabbi on the planet." She wrapped a hand around the tattoo wreath circling her arm. "He really gets what Judaism is about and he's not afraid to say so."

"Are you Jewish?" Ethel asked. The girl was dark, except for the shock of pink in her hair. A few freckles ran across her nose.

"Born and raised."

Close up Ethel could detect a musky, hippie-ish scent. "What are you doing here then?" She looked at the row of earrings lining the girl's ear: a tiny silver dolphin, a turtle, a peace sign, and a Jewish star, not to mention the feather.

The girl tilted her head and seemed to take notice of the tulip motif on Ethel's blouse. "What are you doing here?"

"That's a good question!" Ethel laughed. "What's your name, dear?"

"Rachel." She offered a blue nail-polished hand. "What's yours?"

"Ethel. Ethel Katz." Ethel took her hand. It was warm and strong.

"How do you do, Ethel Katz?" She gave one solid shake, then let go.

"How do you do, Rachel?" Ethel looked into her green eyes, thinking how they matched the shadowed lids that hung over them like awnings. "How old are you, dear?"

"Nineteen. Whatever that means." She shrugged, the top of her spaghetti-strapped shoulder set one feathery earring into motion.

"It means you're nineteen. What else would it mean?" Ethel leaned in closer. "Everyone here is looking for some kind of deep meaning."

Rachel laughed. "You remind me of my gramma."

What a sweet child. Without the pink hair and jewelry, she might look a little like Casey. "That's very nice," she said. "What's your gramma like? Does she know you're here?" Ethel wondered what her gramma would think of all those earrings.

"Oh yeah, she knows I'm here. I tell her everything. She was happy about it. She's a great lady." Rachel reached around her neck for a string of turquoise beads. Hanging from them was a quarter-sized silver locket with a stone in the middle. "Meet Gramma Sylvie," she said, flipping open the locket with her thumb. From the center of Rachel's palm Gramma Sylvie beamed up at Ethel. She had very short white hair and a broad smiling face with a large space between her teeth. She was wearing enormous hoop earrings.

"She looks very nice. But how do I remind you of her?"

Rachel's green eyes widened. "Well, you're here, aren't you? My gramma can hang with the other ladies in her condo, but she doesn't let them get into her head. I mean, she knows what's real." She clicked the locket shut and tucked it inside her tank top.

Ethel wasn't sure what to make of Gramma Sylvie.

"Gramma Sylvie taught me to see God everywhere." Rachel raised her arms in the air as though she were catching flower petals or snow.

"Do you see it?" she asked Ethel. "Do you see the mystery in everything?"

She spun around on her painted toes inside her sandals. Two bangle bracelets fell to her elbow. She stopped and looked around the store. Her eyes had that dreamy look Ethel had seen more than once around the ashram.

"Do you come to see Anandaji often?" Ethel asked with some concern.

"No, this is my first time. I like him, though. I like lots of teachers. They help make life a little more sane. It's insane out there, you know."

Ethel had never thought of this. Was her life insane? She looked at the Jewish star on Rachel's lobe. "And you like Rabbi L'Chaim too?"

Rachel nodded, her earrings bobbed. "Yeah, he's cool. But they're all pretty much the same. They're all talking about the same thing." She shrugged. She looked at Ethel and took a long breath in, letting it out slowly like Debra did when she did her yoga. Then she reached for Ethel's hand and held it in her warm palm. "It was very nice meeting you, Ethel. It really was. It's nice you're here."

"Very nice meeting you too, Rachel." Ethel watched as Rachel turned and skipped through the screened door, which almost caught the rim of her long orange skirt as it closed.

She sighed, wishing Rachel had stayed longer. It would have been nice to take a walk or have some tea, maybe ask a few more questions about Gramma Sylvie. She realized she still had Rabbi L'Chaim's book in her hands. She placed it on a nearby counter holding a rack filled with thin volumes. The books all seemed to blur together, but then one with a colorful jacket caught her eye. It was by someone named Shanti and called, *One Hand Clapping, One Soup Cooking, One Quilt Hanging*. The cover was a beautiful photograph of a patchwork quilt, the sort Ethel had always loved and wished she had the patience to make. She looked at the photo and marveled at the detail of each square of fabric. She opened the book, thinking she might learn something about quilting. Her heart sank when she found the pages filled with more of the same spiritual lingo every other book in the store contained. *Are you separate?* Shanti asked. *Are you defined by the boundaries of your body and mind? No more than one square in a quilt is separate from the quilt, just as a carrot in a soup pot is not separate from the soup.*

Now she was a carrot.

One soup can contain a cornucopia of vegetables, and just as many herbs and spices. This diversity comprises a whole, yet it is only one soup. One quilt is an intricate patchwork of colors and patterns, joined into one continuous fabric to make one quilt. The one essence that enfolds the many into a seamless, unified whole.

Ech, just like the others. Maybe I'll take a quilting class when I get home. Ethel slid the book back into the rack and glanced at the balding fellow turning pages next to her. Down the aisle two women were trying on sweatshirts and laughing at their mussed hair. A girl gingerly sniffed tiny bottles of scented oils. Was she one with these people? Was she one with these books and soaps and pillows? Was she one with Rachel and Henry and Anandaji?

Ethel stepped out the screened door and down the short road that lead from the bookstore to the garden. Stone benches were placed around the garden and goldfish swam in the pond in its center. Feathered clouds floated in the clear, blue sky. An old dog lay in the shade of a young man seated on a bench. She studied the complex pattern of cobblestones along the garden path, the green grass on the manicured lawn, and the lilies lining the garden fence. She gazed down at her newly moisturized feet inside her sandals. Lifting her right foot, she inspected her toes. The second toe was longer than the big toe; the pinkie had a slight curl inward. Five different toes, she thought. Five toes, one foot.

Sixteen

For the rest of the day, Debra wore a silent sign pinned to her T-shirt. Several others had worn these signs throughout the week. Ethel found this unnerving. She disliked their mute, peaceful expressions. It perturbed her that Debra, who was normally so verbal and engaging, now shared this perplexing ritual. People talk. It's what they do. At least Debra had warned her before she donned the badge, pulling her aside after lunch as they headed for the lecture hall, and explaining her desire to stay silent for the remainder of the weekend: more about how she worked all week and how this was her only chance to be quiet with herself. How quiet does a person need to be? Debra did seem tired, and her eyes asked for Ethel's understanding. More than once in the lecture hall, she had reached over to squeeze Ethel's hand.

After the evening satsang, Debra went right to bed. Ethel followed a trail of people to the dining hall for a bedtime snack. She wanted to grab a piece of fruit to bring on her trip home tomorrow. There was some banana bread out, so she sat down to have a slice with a glass of milk. About a dozen people were scattered around the room, either in silence or talking softly. A few kitchen workers were laughing while they mopped the floor and scrubbed counters. Suddenly there was a hush. Anandaji had entered the room. He smiled and headed toward the snack table, put a slice of banana bread on a napkin, and left. All eyes followed him. The poor guy, he can't even get a bedtime snack without everyone staring at him. Ethel had always felt badly for celebrities, imagining that theirs was a strange and lonely existence. She had a feeling that Anandaji, for all his importance with this crowd, dealt with some of this same loneliness. She had an urge to follow him, pat him on the back, and ask him what he thought of the banana bread, and whether he was heading to his bungalow for some Earl Grey. She could wish him a good night's rest. But Anandaji left at a fast pace, clearly not interested in company.

Back in her room, Ethel gathered her things together. This time she knew for certain she was leaving. She folded her Florida sweatsuit into the bottom of her suitcase, collected a few pants and tops hanging in the closet, and checked under the bed for stray belongings. She was thrilled to find her lost lipstick lying in the groove between the carpet and wall, as if it had been waiting there for her to discover it. She thought of calling Fran to arrange a dinner date for tomorrow night, but decided she'd wait. Hopefully Debra would agree to stop for dinner on their way home. She imagined asking Debra the questions that had been circling in her mind: What kept her coming back to the ashram? What made her want to be in silence? What did it feel like not to talk to anyone all day? Ethel was ripe for conversation and good food. She longed for the excitement of the city, people rushing here and there. Enough with all this whispering and meditating. As expected, she wasn't very tired either, but there was nothing to do except go to bed, so she gave it a whirl.

Outside people were chanting in the garden and the Indian melodies flowed through her open window. She could smell the faint perfume of burning incense. She thought of Rabbi L'Chaim and his Sh'ma chapter and wondered if people chanted Hebrew on his retreats. All these hippies growing old and still looking for God. The one God. Ethel pulled the covers close around her and glanced at the clock—only ten thirty and the long night ahead. She had a feeling she'd be spending it thinking instead of sleeping.

Her suspicion proved true. By 2:00 a.m. she'd tossed and turned so often, the mattress pad had balled up under her sheet, and she'd been up to straighten it out twice. She had gone to pee three times and turned over her pillow once an hour to keep the cool side next to her cheek. At this point there was no cool side and though a slight fatigue was trickling in, it was mixed with agitation. Doubting sleep was in store, she got up, dug her sweatsuit out of her suitcase, and headed outside.

The night was cool and misty with a moist breeze. It took a moment for her eyes to adjust to the dim light from the streetlamps, but soon she was walking up the long road that led to Anandaji's bungalow. The gradual incline was her best chance for exercise and, hopefully, exhaustion. On either side of her, the thick woods seemed to reach back forever. Ethel wasn't used to nighttime walks unless it was with Fran and her little terrier, Zip. They'd walk around the well-lit blocks of their condo village, chatting and laughing at Zip, who sniffed and peed on every bush and hydrant. It would be good to do that again. She glanced nervously at the woods and hoped for the bungalows to come into view. Just knowing people were inside them would make her feel more comfortable. There was only a glimmer of a thought that she might actually see Anandaji. It was the middle of the night, after all, and people were always saying how rare it was to win his private audience.

His outline appeared when she rounded the hill, a slight, athletic form dressed in shorts and a windbreaker. He was standing on the porch steps of his bungalow, and his smooth head caught the porch light's reflection. He saw her coming and waved.

Oh dear, what had she gotten herself into?

"Hi Ethel," his voice rang out in the quiet night. "What brings you to these parts so late?"

"I couldn't sleep," she answered. "I thought I'd get some exercise to wear me down." She walked toward him. "How about you?" She stopped just shy of the porch. "Are you always up this late? I heard enlightened people don't sleep much." She crossed her arms in front of her.

Anandaji laughed. There were those eyes of his, twinkling away. "Well, for what it's worth, I usually sleep. I just couldn't tonight. It's kind of neat out here, though. Like being a kid again and breaking the rules."

Ethel chuckled. She wasn't sure she felt like a kid, but she could see that Anandaji did. He bounced a little on the rubber soles of his sandals.

"You must have liked being a kid," she said.

He nodded. "Best time of my life."

"What were you like when you were little?" She tried to picture it: an eight-year-old Anandaji with a crew cut.

"Oh, you know, the usual shenanigans." He sat down on the top step.

Ethel pushed up her sleeves and walked up the steps "Like what shenanigans?" She sat a little distance away and turned to look at him.

"Oh, chasing the neighbor's dog, slicing up worms, getting stuck in trees."

"Oh, I see. You were a little rabble-rouser."

"Yeah, my mom was cool, though," He stuck his legs straight out and flexed his ankles. "She knew how to handle me."

"You were lucky. I wouldn't have been too patient with that stuff." Ethel thought a moment. "I guess you were Robert then." She held her breath, surprised at her gumption in bringing up the name topic again.

"I guess so. It would have been pretty strange if I was named Anandaji, huh?"

She laughed, pleased with his willingness to poke fun at himself. "Did your friends call you Robbie? I could see you as a Robbie." She squinted, trying again to imagine him as a little boy.

"Yeah, they did actually. I always liked that name."

"Me too." She reached down and tightened the double knot on one of her laces. "Were you sad to give it up? When you became Anandaji, I mean."

"Well, by then I was Robert to most people." He looked off into the side yard. A light went on in a bungalow farther up the hill. The peepers were trilling, and it reminded Ethel of her first trip to the country as a girl.

"Come to think of it," Anandaji said, "by the time I changed my name, I kind of felt like Robbie again."

"What do you mean?" She tilted her head and peered at him.

"Well." He shrugged. "Like most people, I had some hard times, years when I felt lost. Those were the Robert years."

Ethel was surprised to hear this. Moths fluttered against the porch lamp, casting a flickering light against Anandaji's face. She found it hard to picture a lost Robert in that happy expression. "I guess the Anandaji years have been pretty different," she said.

"Yes. Lighter. Simpler." He drew his knees up and wrapped his arms around them. "A little more like childhood."

Ethel had always thought childhood might be overrated. After all, what was the use of growing up if all you wanted was to feel like a kid again? She decided to keep an open mind, though.

"Do you feel that way all the time?"

"In a sense," he said. "Deep down."

Ethel studied him. A calm came from his eyes; stillness always seemed to surround him. She wondered whether she ever felt what he did. She wasn't sure.

"Can you describe it more?" she asked.

Anandaji nodded. "You want to get some exercise while we talk? I was just about to take a little walk."

"Sure," Ethel took hold of the railing and stood up. She brushed off the seat of her sweatpants. Anandaji bounded to his feet and trotted down the steps. He's so athletic, she thought. Before she came to the ashram, she never would have imagined he'd be a sports type.

They started down the long dirt incline. Ethel could smell the wet scent of spring. Walking with Anandaji, she did not find the woods so ominous anymore.

"Did you ever go white-water rafting?" he asked.

"Me? That'll be the day."

They both laughed.

"Well, it's one of my favorite sports, and the last time I went I realized what a good metaphor it is for my life now."

"How so?" She examined his stubbly head and wondered what he'd look like with hair.

"Because when you raft you sort of set yourself up for the unpredictable. Even if you choose a lower level, you could find yourself in some pretty rough water. That happened to me when I was just starting out. I signed up for the moderate course. Turned out it was not moderate!"

"Oy, I would have plotzed!"

Anandaji laughed. "Yeah, it got dicey really quickly. But the great thing about rafting is that it makes you stay in the moment. You can't spend time thinking. You have to stay alert, because you never know what's coming around the bend."

Definitely not for me, Ethel decided. The night was beginning to clear, and a curve of the moon showed through the rising mist.

"Mostly things move really quick," Anandaji said. His sandals made a little squeaking sound when he walked. "But even when it's calm, the water still envelopes you; it's the constant, and if you depend on it, take your cues from it, it will guide you through. You learn to trust that it will carry you, no matter what's coming."

"It could also kill you," Ethel said. As soon as the words were out, she half-regretted them, hoping she hadn't hurt his feelings.

Anandaji only nodded.

"That's true," he said. "What's weird about water, though, is that if you get caught in a current, the way out is never to fight it, you just have to take a deep breath and go way down and then you can almost always swim out from under it. But people panic and fight the water. That's how they get into trouble."

When they reached the bottom of the bungalow road, Anandaji led her through a little moonlit trail that shortcut into the heart of the campus. Following him through the dark, she was grateful for the reflector tape on the back of his windbreaker. She thought over what he had just said and when they stepped off the trail, she asked, "Does the water represent God, Anandaji?" She wanted to get all of his meaning.

"You could say that. God or life. There's a trust that no matter what happens, no matter how wild it gets, it'll be okay. Something is buoying me along."

"What about pain?" Ethel asked. She thought of those sad, lonely years after Milt died.

"It's sort of like rough water," Anandaji said. "There's a way to ride it, even enjoy it."

"Enjoy pain? How could that be?"

"It's like that eddy. You can't fight it; you just have to dive deep and accept whatever comes, welcome it. Something changes then."

Instead of going around the garden, they took the path through it. The lilac bush was sweet with fragrance. She thought of the night Henry had found her there and she reached to touch a blossom, still wet from the afternoon rain.

"Are you married, Anandaji? A handsome man like you, I'd expect to see you with someone."

She wondered again at her moxie, but she was proud of herself at the same time. She figured the ashram was filled with people who would give anything to have this conversation, so she might as well take advantage of it.

"Nope," he stepped aside to let her pass through the small garden gate. "Used to be."

He fell into step with her again.

"Oh," said Ethel. "During the Robert days?" She felt suddenly honored by Anandaji's openness, and happy to be with him.

"Actually, she fell for Anandaji. She was really sick when we met. We only had a short time together."

Ethel brought her hand to her mouth, not knowing what to say. This is some amazing fellow, she thought.

"It's okay," said Anandaji. "It's been a while."

He put his hands in his pockets.

"She was lucky to have you," Ethel said.

"And I, her." He watched the ground while they walked, and for the first time all week Ethel saw sadness in his face.

"I know what that feels like," she said softly.

They walked silently for a few moments. A lone star shone in the distance. She scanned the residence hall's darkened windows, wondering which one was Debra's. Here and there a light was on, and she imagined the ashram night owls reading in bed. Henry in wire-rimmed reading glasses or Rachel with her sleep-mussed pink hair.

At the courtyard outside the hall, they stopped and faced each other.

"I want to thank you for something, Anandaji." She touched his hand.

"What's that, Ethel?"

"Thank you for helping me understand Debra. My daughter."

He raised his eyebrows. "Did I do that?"

"Yes."

"Well, okay then," he covered her palm with his own. "You're welcome."

His hand was warm, and he patted hers gently before he took it away.

"I guess we'd better try to get some sleep, huh?"

He nodded toward the residence hall.

"Probably a good idea. You know what?"

"What?" he tilted his head.

"I'll miss you," she said.

"I'll miss you too." He gave her that Sol smile, so playful. "You're fun to have here."

"I know. You said that. I guess there aren't too many like me."

"That's for sure."

Ethel laughed and opened her arms to give him a hug. She had to reach up a little to meet him. He smelled like tea and fresh air, and she was pretty sure she'd never know anyone like him again.

He patted her back and stepped away.

"Goodnight, Ethel," he said.

"Goodnight, Anandaji."

She watched him turn and walk up the slate path toward the garden, then she continued slowly through the courtyard, taking her time, thinking about life and its unexpected turns, feeling the air and the night.

Seventeen

"THE FISH PLACE SOUNDS great," said Debra. "I'm ready for some flesh!"

She bared her teeth for Ethel who let out peals of laughter.

"Oy, I never want to see another bean," Ethel cried.

They were in the parking lot loading their cars. A few dozen people were doing the same, several of who seemed to want to chat with Debra. Ethel waited by her Volvo, rearranging the supplies she'd set in the passenger seat: directions, cell phone, Kleenex, bottled water, an apple from the dining hall, her Judy Collins CD. The day was cooler than it had been all week, but clear, and she looked forward to the ride home through the mountain landscape.

She spotted Henry sauntering through the parking lot and waved him over.

"Hey Ethel," he called, "leaving us so soon?"

"Yes, I am," said Ethel, wondering if Henry ever left this place.

"It's been nice to know you," he said, coming closer. "I hope you come back again."

Ethel flinched a little.

"I don't know about that, but it's been very nice getting to know you too."

She thought of Henry's kindness toward her. There was one of those little alligators on his jersey and he had on the same khaki pants he'd worn all week. She smiled to herself. No one else at the ashram dressed quite like Henry. She was grateful to have had him there. Henry bent and gave her a quick hug, then headed toward the dining hall, leaving Ethel pondering what it might be like for him to return to the hubbub of the world and an empty apartment without his wife.

She looked over at Debra, laughing and hugging a red-headed woman. Several times throughout the week, Ethel had admired this woman's lively manner and flashing eyes. I guess it can go either way, she thought; she won't have any trouble back at home. At the morning satsang, Anandaji had suggested to the weekend crowd, "There's really no difference between the ashram and home. It's all life. In truth, there is no spiritual path. There's only now. It's the mind that perceives time and differences and makes comparisons, determining one thing as better than the other. The mind resists situations and longs for them to change, or resists change and longs for the security of the known. In truth, it's all okay; it all can be welcomed." Ethel thought it funny that while Anandaji was saying this she was thinking how different home would seem to her in light of her days at the ashram. To be around regular people would be a big relief. People who ate meat and wore stylish clothing and would never dream of spending the day in silence. People who talked about everyday things: work, politics, and shopping, instead of God, awareness, and enlightenment. How could he think there was no difference?

Debra got into her Subaru and waved Ethel on to lead the way. Ethel was happy to oblige, seeing as the directions were fresh in her mind. She laughed, thinking how she'd reviewed them every time she'd had the urge to escape home. It made for good reading material considering the slim pickings at the ashram bookstore! She slid into the driver's seat, rolled down the window, and pulled onto the road that headed out of the ashram.

From her rearview mirror she could see the road that snaked up to Anandaji's bungalow. She envisioned him kneeling in his garden, his hands covered with soil. Suddenly there was a lump in her throat and for what seemed like no reason at all, she was crying. She pulled a Kleenex from the pack on the seat beside her, the same pack Debra had given her, and wiped her nose. How silly. What was she now, a gurunick? It's not like she loved this man. She thought of Anandaji's boyish smile and crystal blue eyes and had to admit that his good looks alone would stay with her. What about the rest? What about his warmth and easy manner, the talks they'd had and how relaxed she felt around him? And all those teachings—some of them pretty crazy. But mostly he gave good reminders: accept things as they are—nothing wrong with that—feel your feelings, like Henry had taught her, and don't believe all the nutty thoughts in your head. She could certainly benefit from that. Then there was all that jazz about finding out who you are and everything being one, which she still didn't quite understand.

Ethel looked in the rearview mirror. Her eyes settled on Debra's license plate and she smiled through her tears. "ONE," it said. So now at least she knew why Debra chose that word. She took in Debra's wild, gray curls waving willy-nilly from the wind through her window. Her little "Abraham." Ethel sighed and wiped her eyes. Pop's name for Debra, Abraham with his insatiable thirst to know God. The daughter's thirst had led her mother to the ashram. Or had it? Is that really why she had come?

Ethel signaled left, remembering that the road took a surprising turn up ahead. She thought about the question Debra had asked at the mike that morning. She'd been eager to get up there, waving her arms to catch Anandaji's attention. The question was about peace and why it was so hard to bring the feeling of contentment that she had at the ashram home with her. Anandaji's voice was gentle while he explained how peace was always there, it was each person's truest nature, and it was only the thinking mind that constantly led people away from the here and now and kept them from being aware of it. "But why is it so easy to feel peaceful around you, Anandaji, and not when we leave?" Debra persisted, a real frustration in her voice.

"Because when you are with me, you are just with me," said Anandaji. "And when you leave you are looking for something you think you've lost. You can't lose me," he said, his voice rising, "you can never lose me because you are me. Ultimately you are the only teacher you need. I'm just a stand-in. My job is to remind you that you're the real teacher. The teacher you can never lose. The teacher you bring home with you."

At first Anandaji's intensity had made Ethel fidget in her seat. What a thing to say. You can never lose me. You are me. But as he went on, he made more sense. Their early morning exchange had left her with a trust she couldn't deny. And she liked that part about Debra not really needing him.

They came into a small town and stopped at a light. Turning, she waved at Debra, who waved back and honked lightly. Was it like what she felt for Debra? She'd always love her. Debra could never lose her. She looked in her rearview mirror at Debra's face behind her. She had a gentle, serene look, watching the cars roll by, as if she was having no trouble bringing the peace of the ashram with her. "That's because it's always with her," Ethel said out loud. It's always with her, she thought again.

She looked at Debra and realized that she understood her expression. It was the same feeling she'd first had at Anandaji's bungalow, strangely at home with everything, a sort of peaceful awe. She knew it from other times too:

that day at the beach looking at the shell as a little girl—watching Debra step solidly onto the stage and accept her college diploma—and the time at Milt's grave when she cried so hard nothing was left but an inexplicable calm. That's what Anandaji meant, that's what we can't lose.

She had the feeling Anandaji's teachings were deeper than anything she'd been able to imagine up until now. It wasn't the words. The words weren't enough. Wasn't he always saying that? It wasn't even the look on Debra's face. She took another studied glance at her. It was something behind her face. How could that be? What's behind her face? She recalled a question Anandaji had posed a few days ago, one of those Zen riddles—something like: "What did your face look like before your parents were born?" At the time it had seemed ridiculous. What kind of face could Debra have had before I was born? That's crazy! But now she couldn't help thinking about it. She thought of Debra as a very little girl, her halo of auburn curls and those enormous brown eyes. She pictured her as a newborn, wrapped in the pink cotton blanket she could still remember knitting on those tiny needles in her last month of pregnancy. She tried to imagine Debra even before that, even before she'd been in the womb. Who was Debra, before Ethel herself was born? She glanced back at Debra and right then she saw something in her face she'd never seen before. Something that had probably always been there, but for some reason had been hidden from her until now. What she saw was more vast and mysterious than just Debra. It was as if everything she thought of as Debra was just a small slice of who she really was. Debra wasn't just Debra. Like a bird wasn't just a bird. Like a shell wasn't just a shell. She was something indescribable, something beyond time that didn't belong to Ethel alone but belonged to everyone and everything. For a moment there were no thoughts in her head. Just a kind of space, a peace that seemed to go on forever.

The light changed and they headed onto the highway. Ethel accelerated and Debra kept up with her. Rolling mountains appeared on either side of the road, and she turned toward a breeze through the window. She thought of her salmon dinner coming up, of her mail waiting at the post office, of the questions Fran would ask her about her time away. Oy vey, she'd lied. She bopped herself on the head. She'd told Fran she was visiting Milt's sick cousin! She burst out laughing. Debra sped up and waved as she passed, a wisp of her hair blowing out of the window. Oh, thought Ethel, looking in her mirror, I'll miss seeing her face.

IN GRATITUDE

To my husband Paul for insisting on *Ethel*'s worth when she was only a hope, a silly notion, a seed, and for his steady support and reader's ear through the years of her development.

To my daughter, Rosie, for being the inspiring creative force that she is and for her clear and ever-present sensibilities so apparent in the illustrations that grace *Ethel*'s pages.

To my son, Geremy, for sustaining encouragement and unrelenting devotion to *Ethel*'s reason for being, not to mention spot-on feedback at many important junctures.

To my daughter-in-law, Jenny, for enthusiastic readership and 11th hour affirmation.

To my sister, Holly and niece, Laura, for patiently rooting from the sidelines.

To Jan Frazier's Wednesday night writing group for receiving each weekly installment with open hearts and eager minds, offering immeasurably helpful responses. And to Jan herself for her silent insistent example, nourishing mentorship and pivotal lift out of the dry spell.

A bow of gratitude to Lava Mueller for enduring solidarity, spirited reading and insight.

To Muriel Winter Wolf for keen advice and the sort of confidence boosting only writers can give writers.

To Larry Rosenberg for loving dharmic support and generous endorsement.

To Juli Huss for serendipitous and much appreciated camaraderie from afar.

To Liz Bankowski and Ricky Sarnat for reassuring and thoughtful readership.

To Dede Cummings for heartfelt contributions and for so thoroughly believing in *Ethel*.

To Suzanne Kingsbury—for nurturing *Ethel* as her own, dedicating hours of editing, coaching and bolstering, patient, tactful guidance, thorough workmanship and an uncanny ear that not only buoyed *Ethel* to completion, but brought clarity to the mystery of the writing process and my own transformation.

To Paul Cohen along with Anastasia McGhee and Danielle Ferrara of the Epigraph team for deeply understanding *Ethel* and executing an inspired publishing and designing process that exceeded all expectations.

To my many teachers, living and gone, who have pried open the floodgates, as hard as I've tried to keep them closed.

To Ethel, Anandaji and Debra for choosing life on the page.

CPSIA information can be obtained at www.ICGtesting.com
Printed in the USA
BVOW05s2318090514

352807BV00006B/1/P

9 781936 940677